The Reluctant Patriot

A Novel of the American Revolution

by Roger F. Duncan

Down East Books
Camden, Maine

Cover painting by Christopher Cart

10-digit ISBN: 0-89272-695-4
13-digit ISBN: 978-0-89272-695-0

Printed at Versa Press, Inc., East Peoria, Illinois

4   3   2   1

Down East Books
Camden, Maine
A division of Down East Enterprise, Inc.
Distributed to the trade by
National Book Network, Inc.
Book Orders: 800-685-7962
www.downeastbooks.com

Library of Congress Control Number: 2006924657

Table of Contents

Introduction

On February 15, 1775, His Majesty's armed schooner *Halifax* was wrecked on a rock off what is now Halifax Island in the approach to Machias Bay, Maine. Lieutenant Joshua Nunn was in command and a local pilot was at the helm. The *Halifax* was a total loss.

The subsequent court martial in March 1775 exonerated Nunn, his sailing master, and his entire crew, putting the blame for the wreck on the pilot. The pilot was not present at these proceedings, having "slipped away." He was not named or in any way identified. Who was he? Why did he wreck the *Halifax*?

Naval Documents of the American Revolution gave me a great deal of background in both British and American documents, but no mention of the pilot. Mr. John R. Hailey of Croydon, Sussex, UK, searched the Public Records Office in England and sent me much more information, including *Halifax's* crew list, Lt. Nunn's service records, and a photocopy of the court-martial proceedings, but nothing on the pilot. Dr. Trevor Kenchington of Dalhousie University in Halifax, Nova Scotia, gave me a history of the *Halifax*, a description, and a set of her lines. The above are all ascertainable facts.

Having spent unreasonable time searching for the pilot and having found nothing but interesting background, I invented the pilot. I had three credible alternatives: he was a hot-hearted patriot who wrecked the *Halifax* intentionally; he was grossly ignorant and didn't know the rock was there; or he was tired, in a hurry to get home to Machias, pestered out of his mind by Nunn's continuous questions, and a bit careless. He knew the rock was there, but it was the top of a moon tide and the sea was not breaking on it. I chose the last alternative, as it seemed the most interesting. This book is a construction of the pilot's life with background from many sources, supplemented by pure fiction.

I must beg the indulgence of the people of Machias and of serious Maine historians. This is a work of fiction. I invented my own picture of 18th-century Machias. I changed the name of Burnham's Tavern to the Wildcat Inn. I have used the names of people who actually lived there, but have adapted their characters to my purposes, and I have invented other people.

I gratefully acknowledge the help of the late Robert C. Brooks of Sandy Point, Maine, and the tireless encouragement of Francise J. O'Rourke of Cambridge, Massachusetts. Also many other people in both England and the United States have been interested and helpful. My wife, Mary Chandler Duncan, has been and is a firm support, my severest critic, and dearest friend.

Roger F. Duncan
East Boothbay, Maine

Chapter 1

Lee Shore (1754)

What were Ian MacDonald, his wife Alice, and a dozen others doing standing on the edge of the grass above a stony beach in a March gale? It was blowing hard from the southeast, right on shore, driving rain and sleet and flakes of wet snow so hard before it that they ducked their heads and turned away in the heavy gusts.

Far off shore, the gale drove ahead of it heavy seas, each as high as a house, 200 yards from crest to crest and each moving fast toward the land, the impatient wind tearing the top off and driving it ahead in spindrift. An ocean wave is power in motion, fast, majestic motion, constantly urged on by the insistent gale. As each wave met shoal water, it slowed, tripped, crested, and hurled itself against Bibb Rock. Through the rain and spindrift, Ian could see after every wave white water thrown five feet deep over the black rock. Between the rock and the shore, the surge reformed and smaller waves, urged by the wind, crested, collapsed, and sent white water boiling up the beach, almost to Ian's feet, rattling the rocks as it drew back to try again.

They were watching for a little brig trapped by the gale against the lee shore in the shallow bay between Bald Head Cliff and Bibb Rock.

"Think she'll make it this time, Cap?" asked Ian.

"Don't know," replied Captain Brewer. He spoke with the authority of a skipper who had seen many gales. "A lee shore in a March gale is a hard chance for a boxy little brig like that. Last time she came this way she had to tack just short of the rock, I doubt she can get to windward against this sea and she'll never make it around the cliff on the other side of the bay."

"Look, Ian! Here she comes," cried Alice.

Through the rain and flying spray they could just make out two masts carrying a forestaysail, reefed topsail, and double-reefed spanker.

"She's doin' pretty good," said Cap Brewer.

The little brig was making a gallant fight of it, carrying all the sail she could bear, holding her head up as close to the wind as she could, and meeting every crest bravely. In the troughs, she dropped out of sight. The watchers ashore could see only her masts and straining sails. Then the next grey sea picked her up, showing her deck awash and setting her bodily in shore.

"He's doin' the only thing he can do," shouted Cap Brewer above a gust. "Carry sail. He's holdin' her up to wind'ard pretty good. If he can gain enough to make up for her leeway and the 'scend of those big seas—if nothing carries away . . . Be a near thing, though."

As she came up to the rock, the watchers held their breaths. "She's goin' to make it! I do believe she's goin' to make it. She might just creep by."

"Oh, Jesus, NO!" There was a universal cry. Her forestaysail blew out in rags. She turned into the wind, lost way. The next cresting sea picked her up and slammed her down hard on the rock. The next sea drove her higher and smashed right over her.

The watchers stood silent, helpless. In that boiling surf they couldn't have got a boat off even if they'd had a boat. No one could swim in that white froth, either salvors or survivors, if there were any, and probably there were not, for one great sea after another drew back, crested, and pounded the wreck into the rock.

"There go her masts."

"Those poor fellas. They never had a chance."

"She's the salt brig from Spain they been lookin' for in York, likely."

"Likely."

Already, broken planks, bits of rigging, and deck gear were coming ashore, tumbled by the surf.

"Ian, look there. What's that big thing out there?" asked Alice.

"Don't know. Can't tell what. But it's comin' in, and comin' in."

"I see it now. It looks like a barrel." The mysterious object disappeared briefly behind a cresting breaker, but the next one hove it up in plain sight. "It *is* a barrel."

"Prob'ly wine," ventured one. "They likely stowed a few barrels of wine in among the salt. Salting fish is mighty thirsty work."

"Can't be. Barrels don't float on end."

"This one does." It came closer in and closer, tossed and rolled and tumbled by the surf, but always bobbing upright.

"Well, if it's Spanish wine, I want it," exclaimed Cap Brewer. "Come on, Ian, it's worth a wetting." The next wave to break on the beach hove it up and tumbled it over the rocks on its bilge. Ian and Cap, almost waist deep, braced themselves against the undertow, hung on hard to the barrel, and, as the water drew back, rolled it up the rough beach to the edge of the grass. There was an open hole in the head of it.

"That's strange, ain't it. Can't be wine. Wine barrels have

the bung in the bilge, not in the top." A little water dripped out as they rolled the barrel over.

"Bung's drove in tight. Open her up, Cap." They set the barrel upright. On the head, almost washed off, had been chalked the fish sign and Greek letters.

"That's the Jesus sign. Open her up, Cap." Ian whacked at the top hoop with a rock and Cap pried it up with his knife and pried out the head.

"Well, for God sakes!" Four heads kept Alice from seeing. "What in creation is that?"

"It's a baby! A dead baby, for Chrissakes! Prob'ly drowned, poor thing."

Alice pushed her way in, reached into the barrel.

"No, it ain't dead. See, it's all wrapped up in a feather bed, snug as can be. Wet and shook up, but I believe it'll come around. Poor little thing must be half frozen." She tucked the unconscious little mite inside her cloak and scuttled for home.

Alice ran as best she could along the muddy path through the woods. The gale roared through the treetops, clashed the branches, hurled gusts of snow in her face, and pulled at the cloak she held over the little head. She splashed through puddles, squelched through mud, stumbled through patches of old snow until she had to stop, leaning against a rough old tree to catch her breath.

Ian came plashing after her. "I'll carry the little one," he offered.

She shook her head. "You go on and build up the fire," she gasped. "We're coming." Ian sensed the determination and the urgency in her voice and loped ahead. Alice drew a few long breaths and hurried on through the mud, snow, and gale, looking for the first glimpse of their snug house.

In the warm kitchen, held against Alice's warm breast and covered with a blanket, the little boy opened his eyes, kicked and squirmed, became very much alive, and wailed. Ian watched over Alice's shoulder.

'Now ain't that somethin'," he said. "His folks must a been afeared they might not make it and got him all tucked up in the feather bed, put a chunk of ballast in the bottom of the barrel to float it on end, and left just a little hole for air at the top. When that forestaysail blew out, they knew she was gone, so they chalked the Jesus sign on top and set the little lad adrift, and he came straight to us. Well, I came over the sea, too."

"I think he's going to be all right, and he was sent to us special. Robbie is just getting weaned, so I can nurse the little fella."

"What are we going to call him, Alice? I brought the feather bed home, but there was no note on it nor in the barrel, neither, to say who he was or who his people were. Jesus was written on the barrel, but we can't call him that. The brig was the *Nuestra Signora de Something or Other,* but we can't call him that."

"See," said Alice. "He has a little Saint Christopher medal around his neck. We'll call him Christopher, for 'twas Saint Christopher brought him safe ashore."

And that's how Chris MacDonald got his name.

Chapter 2

Scarborough

Christopher MacDonald, for so he was named, although no court ever decreed it and no birth certificate ever attested to it, remembered very little of his early life. He grew up with his older brother, Robbie. He was a brother if not by blood, then a brother by mutual consent, for the MacDonalds were one family.

The father, Ian, a tall, strong blue-eyed Scotsman, had come to America as a boy of twelve and been apprenticed to a sparmaker in Portsmouth. His master was an exacting craftsman who demanded nothing but the best from those in his shop. Even the rough work of squaring up a mast from a tree three feet in diameter had to be done exactly to the line.

At first, Ian picked up chips, but soon learned to sharpen axe, adze, and plane. When he grew strong enough, he did rough work with the adze, cutting the corners off squared timbers to make them octagonal, the form in which the big spars were shipped to England. By the time he was nineteen, he had learned the trade thoroughly, was declared a journeyman sparmaker, and married Alice.

Ian had met Alice at her father's tavern in Portsmouth, where she drew beer, popped corks, and measured out drams of rum for sailors home from voyages long and short, for farmers in town to sell sheep and corn, and for rowdy apprentices.

Ian, now earning wages as a journeyman sparmaker, caught her eye, took her hand, and off they went to establish a home where Ian found work making spars for small boats from logs rafted down the Ogunquit River.

Alice had learned to read and write, to cook, sew, and keep house. Robbie was born the next year and Chris joined the family without question or official sanction. In his first few years he tumbled about with Robbie, who was bigger and stronger, who occasionally pummeled and mauled him, but Alice was careful to show the same love and care for each boy and to insist that they care for each other.

In 1760, when Chris was six, Henry Moulton persuaded Ian to move to Scarborough and work in his spar shop.

Scarborough smelled of sawn lumber and salt fish, drawing its strength from the inexhaustible forest that pressed in behind it and from the infinite and inexhaustible ocean in front, the two connected by the winding, marshy Nonesuch River. From dawn to dusk the town vibrated to the stamp and rasp of sawmills. Teams of oxen dragged in creaking sledges of logs from the woods, and from the mills came sawed boards and deals. Coopers shaved out barrel staves and heads. Less- skilled men found work making shooks for sugar boxes and splitting out clapboards and shingles. A small brig or schooner was usually in frame at Mills's shipyard, and fishermen built pinkies, sloops, shallops, or skiffs as they felt the need or found the time. There were usually several small vessels at the wharves making up cargoes for the West Indies—sawn lumber and clapboards for houses, barrel staves, hoops, and heads for molasses and rum, shooks for sugar boxes, and slabs of salt fish. Smaller sloops and pinky schooners carried lumber, firewood, and smoked or salted fish to Portsmouth, Newburyport, Salem, and Boston and returned with flour, salt beef, cloth, boots, molasses, and rum.

Through Chris's memories echoed the stamp and rasp of sawmills, the raps of hammers and axes, the warmth of the hearth, and the smell of hot bread. Particularly, he remembered the day he learned to swim. His father had often taken him and Robbie to the beach where they waded and splashed in the warm, shallow water of the river. He held Chris up with one hand under his belly, urging him to paddle and kick.

"We got a lot tied up in you, laddie. I know you'll learn to swim soon, 'cause if you were born to be drowned, you'd never have come safe ashore in that barrel." Robbie had been given the same treatment, but so far, neither boy was a fish.

One summer afternoon with the tide rising over the sun-warmed flats, the boys were splashing about in the shallow water. Chris climbed on a boulder lying on the edge of the channel, flapped his arms, and crowed like a rooster. Robbie waded out and climbed on the boulder. The two struggled for the top and Robbie pushed Chris off into the deep water on the channel side. He went in with a laugh and a splash, went head under, put down his feet, and felt no bottom. Frightened, he scrambled for the surface, came out into the air, and found himself swimming. He paddled to the boulder, hung on for a breath, pushed off and found he could keep his head out and could go anywhere he wanted to. He was floating, weightless, no longer earthbound, exalted. He dog-paddled around the rock and climbed up. Before Robbie could push him off, he jumped off again and swam ashore. The world of waters was his and he loved it.

★   ★   ★

Some of his memories hurt. Like the day at the smoke-house. In the spring of the year, when the alewives swarmed up the river to spawn, thousands were bailed out in dip nets, soaked in salt, hung on sticks, and smoked. The boys carried sticks of alewives into the smokehouse and sticks of golden-brown smoked fish out to be stowed in boxes and shipped out in schooners. Chris did his share, emerging from the smoke-house coughing and weepy-eyed with two sticks of alewives. Sam Libby, who was bigger than Chris, jeered, "Here comes lit-tle Chris, brown as an alewife already, but too small to sell." Robbie swung at Sam, who stepped back astonished, then the two grappled and went down with Robbie underneath. Chris tore into Sam from the side, but before any damage was done, Sylvanus Scott, who owned the smokehouse, pulled the boys apart. Holding Chris at arm's length, he said, "You're a feisty lit-tle lad, aren't you! Why don't you pick on someone your own size?"

Chris didn't understand all he heard, but he knew that the olive color of his skin and his small size set him apart from everyone else as "different" and therefore inferior. He was hurt and the hurt lasted.

He remembered Henry Moulton's spar shop where Ian worked. He went in nearly every day to pick up chips for Alice's fire. He watched Indian John, generally known as Jackie, standing on a long, straight log swinging a broadaxe with a slow, powerful rhythm, taking off a long chip at each swing, stepping back and taking off another, leaving a clean flat face ahead of him.

"Who are you, little feller?" asked Jackie.

"I'm Chris."

"He's my boy," put in Ian.

"Feed him good, Ian. He's got some growin' t'do."

"I'm seven already," said Chris.

"Well, eat hearty, Chris, and you'll grow to be a man yet." Jackie swung his axe again.

Indian John knew little of his own origin. His family had been massacred in one of the Indian wars, and he had been brought up by a Massachusetts family. He had gone to sea while a boy, as cook on a fishing vessel, but persistent seasickness persuaded him to find work ashore. He very soon tired of eating sawdust in a sawpit and acquired sufficient skill with tools to go to work for Henry Moulton. He and Ian worked together and soon became friends. Jackie had few others, for he was an Indian and looked it. One day a loiterer lounged into the spar shop and found Jackie with his adze titivating a spar, rounding it out with gentle short strokes dropping almost transparent chips, and doing it by eye. The loiterer watched a while and arrogantly observed, "That's a good job, a real good job—for a god-damned red Indian."

Ian, broadaxe in hand, blazed, "OUT OF HERE! NOW," and the man fled.

When he wasn't busy, Jackie was friendly to those who were friendly to him, particularly to Ian and Chris and, more distantly, to Robbie and Alice.

One rainy day, Jackie was making mast hoops. The fire under the steam box spread a welcome warmth as Chris fed it chips. Jackie cooked tapered strips of ash in the steambox, then bent them around inside a form to make a hoop that would be riveted when cool. While waiting for another set to cook, Jackie observed, "That's a nice piece of ash we got there, Chris. Not like that bitchy, cross-grained brittle red oak."

"What's ash?" asked Chris.

"It's a kind of tree, but a different tree. It's got a leaf like this," he said, sketching the elliptical shape in the dust, "and usually grows on the edge of the woods near a stream. I found this one up the river near a brook. See how straight the grain is and how straight it splits."

"Bendy," said Chris, trying one of the strips Jackie had cut and tapered.

"That's it. Bendy. But it doesn't break. What the old people used for canoe ribs and bows. That piece is just right for a bow—flat on the outside and rounded on the inside and tapered at the ends. Look." With his knife Jackie notched the ends of the stick. With a bit of the line used for snapping lines on spars, he bent the bow and strung it. "Not good for more than rabbits," he said, "but just your size. I'll make you an arrow."

Chris remembered the launching of the *Two Sisters* at the shipyard. Just before noon when the spring tide was at its highest, everything in town stopped. Even the persistent stamp of sawmills was stilled. A crowd gathered around the new ship, freshly painted and handsome, poised on greased ways, the product of many men's work for months past. The rhythmic crack of mauls driving wedges ceased. Keel blocks were knocked out. The crowd moved forward in anticipation. A big man stepped in front of Chris, so all Chris could see was the seat of a broad pair of pants.

"There you are, little smelt." Suddenly he was lifted off the ground, high in the air, and seated on the broad shoulders of the man standing behind him.

The new vessel began to move, gathered speed, plowed her stern into the water, and floated free. The crowd cheered. Muskets were fired into the air. The vessel caught her balance, floated high in the water, and was warped alongside the wharf to have her masts stepped.

He had other memories of the spar shop. A long spar, roughly squared, lay on blocks. Ian stood about halfway along it, looking at a paper in his hand, then up at the roof, then down at the spar, abstracted.

"What you doin', Pa?"

"Figurin'."

"What?"

"This spar has to be seven-eighths as big up here in the middle as it is where it comes through the deck. You tell me what seven-eighths of twelve-and-a-half is."

"What's seven-eighths?"

"Well, boy, I'll show you." He sat Chris astride the spar about six feet from the butt end and with his knife scratched a mark in the middle of the spar, then divided it into quarters and eighths.

"Those are eighths. There are eight of them. Count 'em."

" . . . 6 . . . 7 . . . 8," counted Chris.

"Now we'll take seven of them. Count 'em." Chris counted out seven of the eight.

"Now we measure." Ian cut a chip to the mark where Chris held his finger. "That's seven eighths. You're seven-eighths of eight years old. Now run along home and tell Ma I'll be home 'bout sundown."

But the memory that cut deepest into Chris's mind, the one he could never forget, was the fire, the big fire the year he turned eight. It had been a hot, dry spring. Ever since March there had been almost no rain. The gardens withered. The pea vines lay down and died. The corn leaves curled. The wind hung in the west and southwest. For a week in June the sky was whitish, although the sun was still hot and people said they could smell smoke, that the woods were burning over in New Hampshire.

Chris was going hunting. He had learned to pull the bow Jackie had made for him and he had one arrow with an iron point. He set off eagerly up the road where the oxen hauled out the wood sledges. He kept a sharp lookout for rabbits and did not notice the increasing smoke. Right before his eyes, a deer and her fawn crossed the road, heading for the river. Now Chris smelled the smoke. He could taste it and his eyes stung. The brush rustled and a young moose stepped into the road. Chris drew his bow, let fly, and hit the moose just behind the foreleg, right where Jackie had told him to shoot. But the bow was made for rabbits and moose hide is tough. The moose made for the river, ignoring Chris, the arrow dangling.

Chris stumbled through the brush after the moose and his arrow, but the moose moved much faster and the boy was left behind, struggling through the alders. He was now breathless and coughing in the thickening smoke. A distant rumble grew to a fierce roaring. A burning branch landed in an alder bush. Now badly frightened, Chris didn't know where the road was, or where the river. He tried to run through the clutching alders, gasped and choked and stumbled, the savage roaring and crackling sound around him, over him. He was too terrified to move.

Then he felt himself being carried, limp over a sharp shoulder, scratched by brush, then a splashing and he was under water. When he got his head out, he saw he was in Jackie's arms, Jackie standing shoulder deep in the river. The smoke was choking thick, the roaring louder. Through the trees he saw fire leaping, saw the top of a pine explode in flame.

Jackie made his way down the river, out of the fire, to the cleared land and the village where a crowd was gathered, backs to the shore, watching the woods explode in smoke and flame. As the fire rushed through the treetops toward the village, the heat became intense. A house across the river from the fire began to smoke. A tongue of fire burst through the roof, spread over the whole house.

"That's Sylvanus's house," someone cried. "It's gone." And as they watched, the house fell in. A sawmill by the river went, then another, and house after house until the fire moved on.

Chris never got over the fire. Often he woke in terror in the night, dreaming of fire. Even the rushing of a gust of wind in the treetops terrified him unreasonably. He would have no more to do with the woods and turned instead to the sea.

Chapter 3

Exploring

The fire raged and roared through the woods at the edge of the town, burned six houses, two sawmills, and a barn before it petered out in the marsh, leaving only stripped and blackened trees, standing spiky or fallen in a tangle on the ashen ground. To a town founded on the forest behind it and the sea before it, the loss of saw logs for ship timber and of tall straight pines for spars was a major disaster.

Three days after the fire, Si Foster and Red Larrabee dropped into the spar shop, apparently by chance. They were an odd pair. Si (Isaiah) was a burly man, six feet tall with arms like a gorilla, a sparkling eye, and a cheery grin, ready to play any card he was dealt in the expectation that it was a sure winner. Red Larrabee was smaller, rather slight and blessed with red hair, a red beard, and a quick wit. They strolled in, each with an outward expression of nonchalance.

"Hey, Ian, whatcha doin'?" asked Si. "Making chips?"

Ian waited.

"Nice-looking spar. Henry around?"

"Gone up town to talk with old King."

"Oh."

Still Ian waited.

"What's he going to do for trees, now the woods are all burned up?"

"Don't know. I hear King has a crew out swamping a road through the burned stuff to good timber."

"That'll take a while. Red and I were out taking a look around. Trees charred and burned, some standing, others laying all over each other in a hid-jus tangle. King lost six oxen when his barn burned. We got to find trees somewhere else."

"Where?" asked Red, as if on cue.

"To the eastward; wherever trees grow close to the shore."

"And raft the logs back here to the mill?" asked Red.

"No. Build a mill where the trees are."

"And ship the planks back in King's ships? Pretty expensive planks."

"No, you red-headed woodpecker. Move down where the trees are and the mills are and build ships down there. Build a whole new town. Why not?" Si said to Red, telling him *It's your turn now. Put it to him.*

"If we found the right place with trees, a mill stream, and marsh hay for the cattle, we could saw boards, build ships to carry them, and do it all ourselves without King taking all the profit. You could have your own spar shop, Ian. You build a good spar. People would come a long way to buy a mast you made."

Jackie left the bench where he had been fashioning the intricate curves of a gaff jaw from a natural-grown oak crook. "Where is this place you been talking about? Or is it all in your head?"

"Jackie, that's the wisest thing I've heard today. Let's go find it!" said Si. "My whaleboat's big enough to take three or four of us down east to look around. Red's a sawyer and knows trees. I've built more than one vessel and Ian knows spar timber. Ian, will you come?"

"I don't know, Si. It means tearing up everything here."

"Then tear it up. Ain't it worth tearing up something to have your own shop? I've hauled anchor and run for it twice already, and it's been worth it both times."

"Better not to close one door 'til you've looked behind the next," said Jackie. "See what you can find down east."

"We got to finish this gaff first—and here comes Henry."

Over a stew of boiled moose meat, Chris listened to Ian and Alice talk. "So they finally got around to it, did they?" asked Alice. "Lizzie said Red had a bee in his bonnet, but wouldn't tell me what it was."

"When they came into the shop, I knew what they came for. Came when Henry was out, too. 'Oh,' says Si, 'Henry not here?'"

"What did they say?"

"Si wants us to pull anchor and build a new town. He's all ready to go and look for a place. Jackie kind of took Si aback. Said to take a look before deciding. So I guess that's what we'll do. Si, Red, and me will go in Si's whaleboat."

"When are you starting?"

"Day after tomorrow, on the high water. I'll need a blanket and prob'ly a change of clothes and something to eat. Si's bringing a keg of salt beef and Red a bag of hard bread and there's still fish in the sea."

"I'll make you a johnnycake big as a jib."

Two days later, Alice, Robbie, and Chris stood with Lizzie and her three, watching the whaleboat out of sight around the first bend in the river.

Ten days later, the three tired men pulled Si's whaleboat into the calm water of Southwest Harbor in the lee of the Mount Desert Hills. It had been a long and fruitless voyage thus far, ending in a hard row against a brisk summer northwester and a head tide in the Western Way.

"Way enough," called Ian at the tiller. "Oars up," and he slid alongside a rough little schooner tied to a spindly wharf. Red passed the painter through the schooner's fore rigging and Ian grabbed the main chains. No one said anything for a minute. Then a head and shoulders appeared over the schooner's rail, a clean-shaven face wearing a cheery smile and a peaked captain's hat.

"Hey, Cap," called Ian. "Mind if we tie up alongside for a bit while we catch our breath?"

" 'Course not. You're welcome. Just get in?"

"Just."

"Hard pull up against this breeze. Where you from?"

"Scarborough," answered Ian.

"Scarborough? Hear they had quite a fire up that way." The speaker leaned his elbows on the rail and looked down into the boat.

"Sure did," spoke up Si. "Like to burned out the whole town."

"You know Dick King in Scarborough?"

"Certain sure we do. He owns the whole place, or what's left of it. You acquainted with him?"

"I bought lumber off him a few times. What brings you fellas so far down east?"

"Looking for a place to build a mill where there's some trees to saw."

"You are? Well, come aboard. Come aboard. Maybe I can help you. What's your names?" Si introduced his crew as they came over the rail.

'Come below, boys. Maybe you could do with a tot of rum after a hard pull. I'm Jones. Ike Jones they call me when

my back ain't turned. I own this little hooker and we're loading boards for Boston." He was all smiles as the four men
crowded into the little cabin and Jones poured generous tots of
red rum out of a stone jug into pewter mugs. "Set down, boys,
and draw breath and tell me where you're bound."

"Well, Captain Jones, we don't rightly know." Si, as usual,
was doing all the talking. Ian said nothing, studying Jones attentively. Captain's hat, linen shirt, seaman's jacket, silver belt
buckle, duck pants, sea boots. He studied the pewter mug, one
of a set of four and elegantly crafted. And the rum was good
Jamaica rum, not third-run Medford red-eye. He does well in
the lumber business, figured Ian, and is proud of it and proud
of being a seaman, too.

Si was still rattling on. "What we need? Well, I'll tell you
what we need, what we got ordered up there." He looked up
toward the deck beam overhead and beyond it. "What we need
is a river with lots of good pine woods along it, some particularly tall and straight ones for spars and masts. The river's got to
have current enough to run sawmills even in dry times and be
deep enough to bring vessels up to the mills. And then it has to
have meadows and salt marshes growing hay enough to feed
the cattle we need to skid the logs to the water. So far we have
seen lots of trees, but not much else."

Red nodded.

"Well, boys," said Ike, rubbing his hands together, "let me
fill up those mugs and I'll tell you something you'll be glad to
hear." Ike was generous and, on an empty stomach, the rum had
considerable authority. "Down to the east'd there's just that
river you ordered. It's called Machias—some Indian name, I
guess. It's made to order: river, trees, and hay. With a fair
sou'west breeze, you can be there tomorrow night. You go look
at it and then come back and see me."

"We'll do that!" Si almost shouted. "T'morrow."

"Hold a turn on that, Si," spoke up Red, looking sharply at Ike. "You been there?"

"No, I haven't. But I have a mill at Milbridge and another at Chandler's River and I know the country."

"Who lives there now?" asked Red, setting his mug down on the locker.

"Why, no one. Before the war there was a few Frenchies, but they're all gone now. It's all English territory."

"So if there's no one there, how do we get deeds to our property?"

"Ho, my boy, don't worry about deeds. No one in that wilderness will care whether you have a deed or not. I'll give you deeds and get them stamped by the court in Halifax."

"If it's such a wilderness and so far down wind to the east-'d, who is ever going to buy our lumber?"

'Noow," said Ike slowly, "Mr. . . ."

"Larrabee—but most folks call me Red."

"Of course they do. Now I'll tell you what. I'll buy your lumber, shooks, staves, clapboards, and all the firewood you can load aboard my vessels. Why, Red, Boston is crying for wood. They've cut down all the trees within miles of the city and will buy all they can get. And what they can't use they will ship to the Spanish main and the wine islands for sugar, molasses, rum, indigo, coffee—yes, and port and Madeira. There's more gold in sawmills than in King Solomon's mines. I tell you, you can't lose with a sawmill."

"Sounds good. What do you say, Ian?"

"I say we better go look at it. Start at first light. Wind'll likely be northwest in the morning."

They went, they looked, and to their surprise they found it much as Ike had described it. It was a long pull back to

Scarborough, but a few decent northerlies and a dry easterly got them back to Scarborough on a warm, foggy day in September.

Chris dug his clam hoe into the mud, jerked the clod into the hole in front of it, tossed four fat clams into his hod, and straightened up. The mud merged into the gray water and into the gray fog. He heard the thump-clunk of oars on thole pins. A shadow materialized into a whaleboat with the familiar figure of Red at the tiller, Si and Ian at the oars. Chris dropped his hoe, left the hod for the coming tide, and pelted up the shore.

"Ma, Ma! Pa's home! He's here! He's home!"

A crowd had gathered under the low ceiling of the tavern's gathering room. Si, voluble as always, told of their frustrating voyage down east, the fortunate meeting with Jones.

"Jones? Ike Jones? I know him," broke in Richard King. "Came here buying boards and firewood a few times. I know him. He's a fox. He offer to fit you out and you pay him in lumber? Take that and you're in debt to Jones and he'll own you lock, stock, and barrel."

"Well, half of us here are in debt to King," spoke a voice from the end of the far table.

"I'm not pressing anyone to pay right now," put in King. "We'll have to finish cutting an ox track through the burn to where there are good trees and then we are doing business again selling lumber and building ships, same as before. The store can carry you until then."

"Who owns the store?" asked the voice from the end of the table.

Si stood up and banged his mug down so the ale splashed

over his hand. "That river was made for us. Plenty of trees right next to three branches of the river. A fall of water even in a dry summer like this. Sloping banks for shipways and hay enough to feed all the cattle in New England. God Almighty has been saving it for us and it would be a sin to let it go."

"God Almighty doesn't write deeds," said the voice.

The meeting grew louder and more boisterous until the low ceiling could no longer contain it and it broke up.

During the long fall and winter there were many more tavern conferences and family councils. Alice was eager to go, but Ian held back at first. "Who will ever come way down east for a gaff or a boom or a topmast? There are plenty of good sparmakers this side of Cape Elizabeth," he objected.

"People will come a long way for a spar they can count on." said Alice. "Also," she added, for she was a canny one herself, "you will find spar trees close to the river and not have to skid logs two miles through burned woods behind one of King's oxes before you even start to work. And for spars under fifty or sixty feet, Jones can carry them on deck. With Jackie to help, you could have the best spar shop in New England. Here you work for Henry and he gets the profit."

"How about the boys? There won't be a school in the new town."

"I've already taught them to read a little. Robbie is doing quite well. Chris knows his letters and is catching on quick. I can do it." When Jackie agreed to come too, the decision was made. With the same precipitation with which he had married Alice, moved to Kennebunk, and on to Scarborough; with which he had joined Si and Red on the whaleboat voyage, Ian decided to go to Machias.

In one of the first warm days in April, thirteen men went

aboard Tom Buck's schooner *Two Sisters*. Westbrook Berry had his wife and three children and Red Larrabee's wife Lizzie came with their three. They cast off the lines to the wharf and dropped down the river on the first of the ebb tide before a fair westerly breeze.

Chris, now eight years old, stood on Woodin Foster's anvil at the rail, holding on by the main rigging. They were clear of the river and Chris felt for the first time the gentle heave of the offshore sea, smooth and powerful. He felt the clean breeze blowing over miles of clean, cold salt water, heard the swish of the bow wave, the passing of green water alongside, the bubbling of the wake. Through the taut after shroud, through his hands, into his sensitive subconscious passed the subtle vibrations of a vessel under sail. He looked eastward at the hard line of the horizon and never looked astern.

Chapter 4

Townsend

All was not quiet around him, however. Tom Buck, the skipper, having conned *Two Sisters* out of the river, had turned the tiller over to Dan Fogg, perhaps because Dan's short pipe and assured air inspired confidence. Tom was busy clearing his decks of the confused scultch of tools, household gear, and kegs of pork, flour, and molasses.

"Sam and Sylvanus, you two get those blankets below before they get wet. Joe Bonney, stow your saw blades and mill castings right down on the ballast and that bundle of axes on top of them. Woodin, get that little boy off your anvil and lash it to the foot of the foremast. Help him, Jackie. Dan and Ian, lash that God-forgotten heavy old canoe in the fore and main rigging on the port side. Westbrook, what in blazes are we going to do with your cow? Can't put her below. Belay her painter to the lee rigging and milk her, for God's sake, if that's what she's bawling for."

Chris was summarily displaced from his perch on the anvil and set to dragging Alice's iron pot along the deck to the hatch.

Tom had spread hay on the ballast as an accommodation to his passengers. Lizzie Larrabee herded her three children into the after port corner of the hold clear of the hatch and more or less penned them in with blanket rolls, a keg of molasses, and one of flour. Ian and Westy Berry set up their own family enclaves by the forward bulkhead. By sunset the decks were clear and blankets spread on the hay below.

The iron pot disposed of, Chris started aft to see what Dan was doing at the tiller, but before he got there, Si scooped him up and set him astride his neck.

"Come with me, little smelt, and we'll not be under foot." Si set him down on the foredeck, back to the anchor windlass, and bade him stay put. He watched as the wind eased off, the sky faded from blue to gray, the sea smoothed out and reflected on its pearly gray surface the red smudge of the sun setting behind a bank of dark clouds. He shivered and went below to a supper of corn bread and still-warm milk, which Sally Woodin shared with the Larrabees and MacDonalds.

During the night the wind came in southeast and then east. *Two Sisters* heeled to port, sliding the passengers in a heap to the port side, and she began to pitch heavily into a head sea. About midnight, with a thrashing of canvas and a flogging of blocks, she tacked, and everyone slid over to starboard. The little Berrys, upset and frightened by the noise and motion in the darkness, began to cry. Red and Lizzie held their three between them. Chris and Robbie, comforted and reassured, almost went back to sleep. Someone aft was seasick and the disease was catching. Altogether, it was a thoroughly miserable night, made no better when Tom tacked *Two Sisters* again to the north before dawn.

The day was little better at first. There was no hot food. Rain squalls brought annoying leaks in the deck, but by noon the wind hauled more southerly and eased off, the sea smoothed out, and *Two Sisters* could steer a northeasterly course for Townsend. In the afternoon of a cloudy day, she slipped up the quiet harbor and anchored.

The passengers sorted themselves out. Robbie and Chris

retrieved the iron pot from among the Berrys' gear. The very unhappy cow, half strangled by her halter on the port tack and soaked with cold salt water on the starboard, was on her feet again and given several handfuls of hay, but returned very little milk.

Almost before the anchor took good hold, Jackie was standing on the rail by the fore rigging, searching the shore for his sister Nomi. "That's the house over there behind the fish flakes," he told Alice. "As soon as we can get ashore, we'll go and see her and little Ruthie too, and Al if he's home."

"How old is Ruthie?" asked Alice.

"About seven by now. A little younger than Chris and Robbie. Here comes someone out to meet us."

A skiff bumped alongside. "I'm Jim McCobb. Where are you folks from?"

"Scarborough," answered Jackie

"Need anything?"

"You might set us ashore if you have time"

"Glad to. Pass the little fella down."

"I can make it myself" Chris was over the rail and hanging from the fore chain plates before McCobb could move.

"Where's Robbie?" asked Alice anxiously.

"Catching cunners over the stern with Jerry Larrabee," said Ian. "He'll be all right."

Once ashore, Jackie led the way to a neat, low, log house across the road from what seemed like an acre of fish flakes partly covered with drying codfish. Before Jackie had crossed the dooryard, a young Indian woman with glossy black hair in braids around her head ran to meet them and embraced Jackie with enthusiasm.

"Oh, John, it's so good to see you," she burst out. Where

have you been? And where bound? Sit and tell me all about it."

"Scarborough, working for old Henry Moulton ever since you married Al, making chips with this Ian here. This is Ian MacDonald and Alice. This is my helper, Chris."

"Ruthie, come out from behind that door," called Nomi. A sturdy little girl, brown and smiling shyly, came into the light. "This is Chris." Nomi held the door open and the grown-ups went in, leaving Chris and Ruthie looking at each other. There was a silence.

"That your wharf?" asked Chris.

"It's my Pa's."

"Who's your Pa?"

"He's Al McKown. He's out fishing now."

They crossed the road, headed toward the shore between the fish flakes. Chris picked up a flat stone and skipped it across the water. It skipped five times before it sank. Ruthie picked up another and skipped it five.

"Here comes Pa now," cried Ruthie, much relieved to have something to talk about. She pointed at a stoutly built open boat sailing gently up the harbor before the light southerly breeze in the brightening afternoon. Ruthie ran ahead, pattering down the wharf, Chris following.

Al luffed alongside the wharf; passed a line to Ruthie, who dropped a neat hitch over the slender piling, a move that Chris did not miss. Al tripped the sprit out of the snotter, wrapped boom and sail around the mast, and looked up cheerfully, a strong man, young for his years, with the bright blue eyes of his Scotch-Irish ancestry.

"You done good today, Pa," called down Ruthie, noticing the pile of green and white codfish amidship with a couple of blue haddock on top.

"Sure did, little mate. Forty-three codfish and some of them pretty good size. Kept two haddock for us. Who's your friend?"

"His name's Chris. Uncle John came in that schooner over there. Chris came with him. They're all up to the house now."

"I'll go up soon's I get these critters dressed out."

Chris and Ruthie climbed down into the boat and watched Al gut the big codfish, cut off heads, and rip out back-bones. They took turns washing the flattened fish over the side and heaving them up on the wharf. A big codfish came on Ruthie's turn, about all she could manage. Chris reached to help her, but she turned her back, gave it an extra heave, and got it up.

"I'm seven years old. I can do it myself"

"Well done, mate. You'll be an able fisherman yet. Had a big fire down your way, didn't you, Chris."

"Yes."

"We smelled the smoke of it. Were you in it"

"Yes."

"Scare you some?"

"Some." Chris offered no more comment, and Al, sensing his reluctance, dropped the subject. He finished the last fish, tossed it up on the wharf; grabbed Ruthie by the shoulders and slack of her dress and slung her up after it. Chris hurriedly jumped for the ladder and Al followed, grinning in recognition of Chris's independence.

The conference in the house dealt with Jackie's and Ian's work, the arrival of Christopher in the barrel—"I'll show you the barrel if you don't believe it," said Ian—the fire, and the plans for Machias, concluding with the previous night's misery.

The evening was cheery and convivial. Alice and Nomi

shared their varied experiences and agreed to do a baking. The next day Chris and Ruthie lugged wood for the oven, saw Al off to go fishing, and played around the shore. The following day, with a fair wind, *Two Sisters* resumed the voyage to the eastward.

Chapter 5

Machias

The fair wind did not last long, and the rest of the voyage was more miserable than its beginning. Chris remembered the cold wind, the stinging rain, and the march of gray-headed seas, every one of which cuffed *Two Sisters* as it passed. He could get out of the wind by going below, but it was a wet, stuffy, little hold at best and crowded with tired and miserable people.

The wind hung in the east and northeast. Tom Buck held *Two Sisters* hard on the wind, beating into it, but when it settled into the northeast and began to build into a serious gale, Tom decided to up helm and run for shelter. Chris remembered the relief with which *Two Sisters* greeted the change of course as Captain Tom headed for a snug little cove, The Hop Yard, in the dark and gusty afternoon. Chris also remembered the earthquake shock with which *Two Sisters* came down hard on a ledge, stuck, and heeled far to starboard. Each sea lifted her and pounded her down hard on the rock. There followed a great deal of apparent confusion, in which Chris saw a shallop launched, an anchor taken out, and a lot of heaving and hauling around the starboard pin rail.

The pounding stopped as the schooner came upright and, after the tide came, slid off and swung to her anchor, rolling heavily. Then came another jolt and bang and more confusion in the dusk. There was a crowd with a lantern by the port main rigging. Chris couldn't see what had happened at first, but it appeared that the heavy dugout canoe lashed in the rigging had parted its lashings, fallen on the neck of Westy Berry's cow, and killed her. Finally, in the rainy, ragged end of the day, with a coming tide, Captain Tom brought *Two Sisters* into the smooth water of The Hop Yard.

The Hop Yard was heaven: A quiet night, a sunny day, a big fire ashore, dry clothes, the smell of roasting meat, and enough of the unfortunate cow for all hands. This sacrifice to Poseidon brought two days of fair winds and quiet nights at anchor, for no one aboard was well acquainted with these eastern waters. Last came a gentle sail under a showery sky up Machias Bay, with the land closing in on both sides to a quiet anchorage among three hills.

The next day was a muddle of pouring rain, with another grounding—this one a gentle one in the mud—then a small boat, and a shivering shelter under a lean-to of planks laid on a fallen birch tree. They had arrived.

Growing up in a new town was certainly eventful. After rigging a rough shelter for his family, Ian helped set up the double sawmill and Jackie joined in getting out logs to feed it. Before cold weather, Ian had built a tight house of planks and sawed timbers. Chris helped by digging clay from the flats for the stick-and-clay chimney that stood over the open fire.

1764

Besides the Berrys and the Larrabees, there were several other children in the growing town, including a large and very active clan of O'Briens. Near the river bank below the

MacDonald's house grew a clump of birch trees. One warm day in late spring, Robbie climbed one, remembering the sport of swinging birches he had seen in Scarborough. As he shinned up the slender trunk, others came to see what was up. Higher he climbed, getting what help he could from slender branches that broke off under his feet until he was as high as he could go and his weight made the tree sway perilously. Then, holding on by his hands, he swung out with his feet. The supple tree bowed down under his weight, set him lightly on the ground, and swished up again. Morris O'Brien was the next to try.

It was scary going up. "Higher, Morris, higher," cheered the boys. "You'll never get her down from there." Everyone yelled and laughed. Morris scrambled higher, looked down, clutched the tree.

"Higher, Morris, higher!" They all shouted together. The tree was small where Morris was and the bark was slippery. It began to sway dangerously. It was a long way down to the upturned faces and the open mouths shouting, "Higher, Morris." He tried, gained a foot. He would have liked to quit, but the shiny little trunk was so slippery, and the tree swayed all one way. His feet slipped, the tree bowed gracefully and, to his breathless delight, set him down on his feet amid cheers.

"Hey, that's fun," said Morris. "You try it, Sam." Sam was a little doubtful, but tried another tree. Again there were cries of "Higher, higher," but Sam had gained confidence and was set down the same as Robbie and Morris.

At his turn, Chris went up his tree like a squirrel and got high enough to get into the short bushy branches near the top before the tree got too tiddly.

"Swing off!" shouted Robbie. "Let 'er go, Chris." Chris held on with his hands, swung out with his feet, and the tree bowed down, but not far enough. Chris was left hanging by his hands high above the ground, his face in the birch brush and the slim trunk leading up from his hands. He was too high to let go and he couldn't hang on for long. Robbie saw his trouble, jumped up, and grabbed one of the small branches near the top of the bowing tree, put his weight on it, and the tree bowed more. Another came to help and the tree bowed enough so Chris could drop through the small brush at the top of the tree and land with a jolt. The tree swished back derisively and left one very small boy in a humiliated heap on the ground with six bigger boys shouting "Shrimpo!" Trees were not for Chris.

1766

Ian gave Chris a small axe so he could cut firewood and split kindling. With a quick hand and a sure eye, Chris could split kindling to toothpick size. On a mild September day he sat on the chopping block scrubbing the edge of his beloved axe on the whetstone borrowed from the shop. Ian and Robbie stopped a moment to watch.

"Come with us, Chris, and give your sharp-toothed friend something to bite on," said Ian. "We're going for a mast tree and you can help limb her off."

How could he say no?

The wood road over which oxen skidded logs to the mill was now wide and well worn. After a quarter of a mile, Ian said, "Let's go in here. Likely up on the edge of the ridge we'll find what we came for." He struck off to the left over ground springy with pine needles and free of underbrush in the deep shade. Chris felt the tall, dark pines close in around him. However, he followed Ian and Robbie stoutly. Deeper they went into the woods. Chris followed very close behind his father. Ian moved more slowly now, inspecting each likely tree, looking for a straight one about eighteen inches thick with few branches.

Robbie stopped at one taller than its neighbors. "How's this one, Pa?" Ian studied it a minute.

"Looks pretty good, Robbie, but she'll get hung up. No place for her to fall. Don't want to lumber half the ridge to get her out." A little later Ian swung his big double-bitted axe into another. "This one's the one, boys. You lay that small stuff down to make a cushion for her to land on while I start in."

Chris started on a six-inch spruce on the edge of a clearing made by the fall of a huge pine in a winter gale long past. His sharp little axe bit out clean white chips, in which, however, he took no satisfaction. In the woods he felt shut in, his escape cut off; but he got the little tree down and laid it where it would help cushion the fall of the new mast. Robbie, a year older and a bigger boy with a bigger axe, was working on his second little tree.

A gust of wind swished through the forest. Chris stood very still, alert, holding his axe handle hard. Nothing happened. The steady whack of his father's axe was reassuring. Chris got hold of himself and started on the next little tree.

During the rest of the morning, the boys cleared a path for the mast tree and laid a "cushion" for it to fall on. It was no feather bed but a tangle of interlaced smaller trees and brush. Climbing through it, Chris felt his ankle caught in a crotch. He yanked to pull it out, stumbled, grabbed at the butt of a sapling close by and yanked again. He was trapped! Panic washed over him, but he got hold of himself, wriggled free, and went on with the job, shaken.

"Well done, boys," said Ian. "That should take care of her. Lunch time." They cleared a place at the foot of the big tree. The boys collected dry sticks from a dead spruce while Ian kindled a fire from his tinder box. He soon had a brisk little blaze under his tea kettle and broke out a lunch of bread and cheese.

A gust of wind blew a puff of hot smoke at Chris. He choked, coughed, started back, actually ran a few steps, and sat down as far to windward of the fire as he could get.

"What's the matter, Chris?" laughed Robbie. "Don't you know that smoke always blows toward the handsome man?"

After lunch, Ian called Robbie. "Give me a hand, lad, and we'll put this one to bed right soon." Robbie picked up his light axe and stood facing his father next to the tree. Ian swung his axe, took a yellow chip out of the deep scarf. While he was drawing back to strike again, Robbie struck. So they struck alternately, each as the other drew back. Every boy in Machias learned to do this, for lumber was the life of the town.

With the rhythm of chopping in his ears, Chris buried the fire thoroughly and waited for the tree to fall. The sky had clouded over and a warm southwest breeze rustled through the tree tops. Chris felt something awful was going to happen—soon. He felt he'd better get out of there. Hesitantly, he said, "Pa, I'm going home. I got to . . . " he sought for an excuse. Ian sensed the urgency in the boy's voice. He didn't want Chris to give in to whatever was possessing him and he didn't want him to go off in the woods alone and upset.

"Oh, stick with us, Chris. We've almost got her now. You and Robbie whack away at the scarf a little more and I'll start the back cut. She'll come in another fifteen minutes." He picked up Chris's little axe and handed it to him. He found a log for him to stand on across from Robbie, for Chris was too short to chop effectively at the scarf that Ian had started. Robbie laid into his first stroke hard. On Robbie's back swing, Chris struck but with no great conviction. Robbie struck again and Chris struck harder. As the rhythm picked up, Chris put more into it and the chips flew on both sides of the tree while Ian laid into the back cut.

"The boy will make no lumberman, Alice," said Ian that night. "He was nervous about something as soon as we got into the woods and wouldn't get near us at lunch. He chopped away at clearing a path for the tree like a good one, and when I put him to chopping with Robbie, he did very well for one his size, but in the middle of the afternoon he wanted to go home. Looked as if he wanted to run home."

"You notice, Ian," said Alice, "that when he goes for firewood, he always goes to the shore for driftwood before he goes to the woods? He's a water dog, Ian, and no lumberjack. He came out of the water and on the water he'll live.

Chapter 6

Chris Builds a Boat

The summer he was thirteen, Chris built a boat. His horror of the woods and his affinity for salt water led him to be an odd and independent little stick, scorned and often derided by the community as "Shrimpo." He went about his own business by himself.

One smoky day in late May he found his own business to be fishing. He borrowed a bateau from Red Larrabee and started down the river on the ebb tide. The southwest wind came up the river in sharp gusts, making dark catspaws on the water. The marshes were just beginning to turn green and the woods, not yet fully leafed out, were shrouded in a golden mist of new leaves. Chris put his weight on the oars and drove hard into the wind. He felt strong and ready for what came.

As he emerged from the shelter of the river, he felt the full force of the wind hurrying the seas up the bay, cresting them up, and driving their tops off. The bateau, built for smooth water, bucked and rolled, drove her bow under and took a big drink of cold salt water, which swashed aft around Chris's ankles. She reared up on the next sea, stood still despite Chris's strong stroke, slammed down, and took another drink over the starboard gunnel. Chris felt the power of the wind and sea against him, indifferent and overwhelming. Then a smooth patch came. Chris spun the bateau as quickly as he could, but she was a clumsy, unstable craft and took another sea over the port side.

With the wind behind him, even with the tide against him, he was soon in the sheltered water of the river. He grounded the bateau in a sandy cove, bailed her out with a birch-bark scoop Red kept in her, and drew breath. It was no day to go fishing in a bateau. It was a long pull home against the tide, but as he pulled up the river between the spring woods and the golden marsh grass, he determined to build his own boat, more stable and with higher sides.

Si, a shipbuilder by trade—if he could be said to have only one trade—was going mate with Ike Jones in Ike's boat *Polly*. They had just returned from Boston with a cargo of supplies and tools and had left her alongside the mill wharf. Si was on his way home. He had always liked Chris, his "Little Smelt," and had watched him grow into a strong, independent 13-year-old. As he was walking home, he found Chris by the shore, looking at a newly-sawn pine board more than a foot wide. Several others were piled nearby.

"What'cha doin', Little Smelt?"

"I'm going to build a boat and go fishin', but I don't know just how to start."

"You can't go fishin' in one of these skimming dish bateaus they have on the river. What you need is a shallop—but that would take you a long time to build and you'd need more planks than you got there."

"And I want her to be flat-bottomed to pull up on the shore and get over the Starboard Island bar, except at the bottom of the tide. It's got to be a bateau."

"A bateau's too tiddly to fish from and too low in the

water. She'd slop every other sea aboard and she'd be a bitch to row against a chop."

"I know," said Chris. "I was down the river in Red's bateau day before yesterday. But couldn't I make her wider on the bottom so she wouldn't be so tiddly?"

"Why, yes, you could!" Si seemed to take fire at the idea of a new kind of boat. He picked up another plank and laid it down alongside the first. "We could cleat them together—or we could cut them out both the same and then cleat them together and caulk the seam."

"What can we do for a frame in the middle? Shouldn't she be a little round-sided?"

"Let's go look where they're cutting firewood and see if we can find some crooked oak that would be about right." Si started up the path toward the mill. Chris had to run to keep up.

The next day, with Si's help, Chris lined out the double-ended shape for the bottom of his new boat. "You'll notice, Little Smelt, that everything that swims in the sea or flies through the air is double-ended," observed Si.

Si went off with Ike aboard *Polly* the next day. Chris sawed out the two bottom boards and, under Jackie's eye, planed a caulking seam between them. When Si came back, he and Chris found some natural oak crooks in the firewood pile and Si convinced Ike to let Chris have them at firewood prices. Jackie helped shape them up and set up a midship frame. It was a great day when Chris, Ian, Si, and Jackie bent around the four side planks and fastened them with nails Si had brought from Boston. The planks did not quite come together at the stern, so the stern came out triangular. Not long after, there was a launching. Alice poured a libation of rum on *Alice*'s stem and a more generous one in the cups of all who had worked on her. Chris got aboard and seated himself at the oars. Anyone who could get a hand on the gunnel joined in giving her a big shoot out into the river with loud cheers and Si shot off his musket.

The next day, Chris shoved his new boat down the beach and headed down the calm waters of the river. The new boat was a little awkward, as all new things are. The sides seemed too high and the oars too short, but she slipped down the river quickly with the tide. Once out in the bay, abreast of Bucks Harbor and beyond Bird Rock, Chris dropped his new killick over the bow, baited a hook with a clam, and dropped it over the side. It was not long before a big codfish found the clam. Chris had to stand to haul the big critter to the surface. The new boat tipped some, but her high side supported her and Chris wrestled the big fish over the gunnel. In a couple of hours he had a full load of green codfish and blue haddock. By this time the tide had turned and a chill southerly breeze made it an easy row home.

The next morning, after he had swept out the spar shop, carried chips and firewood into the kitchen, and been congratulated again on *Alice*'s good looks and seaworthiness, he took Robbie's lunch basket and three big codfish in his new boat across the river to the mill wharf. Robbie was working at the mill, stacking boards outside with Little Red Larrabee. Dan and Sam Weatherbee were working inside, bundling shingles. The mill had been stamping and the saws coughing back and forth to each other since early morning.

Chris rowed proudly, catching each stroke firmly in the water, pulling through with a jerk of arms and back and admiring the wave *Alice* was making. He grounded her gently on the stony beach beside the wharf, pulled her up as far as he could, and tied the painter high on a piling, for the tide was coming. He took one codfish and Robbie's lunch up the bank. Robbie and Foxy—so-called because, like his father, his hair was red as a fox—already had two piles of 10-foot boards with sticks between the layers for ventilation. These boards had been pine trees only a week before.

"Thanks for the lunch," said Robbie, "and how's the new bateau go?"

"Like a mackerel, but she's no bateau. She's a lot better. And her name's *Alice* and don't you forget it."

"How better?" asked Foxy. "She looks high-sided and clumsy to me."

Chris didn't want any arguments so he went on into the mill looking for Ike. He found him with sawdust in his hair helping Joe Bonncy, the millwright, sharpen a saw blade.

"See you got a new boat," said Joe between strokes of the screeching file. "Who built her?"

"I built her myself."

"Looks like it," said Joe sarcastically.

"What's that you're draggin' around with you?" asked Ike.

"That's a fine big codfish I caught yesterday to pay you for some of the boards you gave me for the boat."

"That's a good boy, Chrissy. An honest man pays his debts right off. I'll mark it down in the book, 'Chris MacDonald. 1 codfish, paid on account.' Take it up to the house and give it to Agatha in the kitchen."

As Chris went out through the shed, he passed Sam and Dan counting and bundling shingles.

"Hey, Shrimpo, where'd you get that bateau you came over in?"

"I built it, and it's no bateau."

"What'd you do that for, you wood butcher?"

"To catch fish." Chris tried to walk by the two, but Sam had to get his shot in.

"It's just a great floating hearse. Paint her black and hire a horse."

Chris fled out the door and up the path to Ike's kitchen. Ike's daughter, Agatha, about sixteen, was peeling potatoes. She wore a neat dress, the colors unfaded. She sat on a stool, a pot between her knees, a little miffed that a young lady should be set to peeling potatoes.

"What do you want, you little shaver?"

"Here's a codfish for you,' said Chris.

"What do I want with a stinkin' fish? Throw it on that locker over there. No, don't. It'll stink up the whole house. Leave it on the step outside. Maybe a gull will fly away with it and with you, too. You stink as bad as the fish."

Chris went back to his boat, afloat by now, pushed off, and rowed up to the store wharf. He was rather discouraged by the reception *Alice* had got at the mill, but he knew she was a good boat and no bateau, even if she leaked a bit. He tied her to the top of the ladder and carried the two fish into the store. Two men were sitting on a bench discussing ownership of marsh hay and paid no attention to Chris and his fish. Chris approached Mr. Steven Jones, the storekeeper and nephew to Ike, generally known as Steve.

"Mr. Jones, here's two codfish I caught for you on account." Chris was pleased with "on account," which he had acquired from Ike that morning.

"On account of what, Chrissy?"

Chris didn't really know what "on account" meant but quickly thought back to the conversation with Ike. "On account of we owe you for flour and stuff."

"Smart lad! Hear that, boys? He's the boy who built that high-sided scow down to MacDonald's."

"That shit cart? What's she good for?

Chris was out the door before Steve answered, stoutly, "To catch fish." And held one up.

When he grounded *Alice* in front of his house, Ian came down to help him pull her up above high water mark. They pulled together, man and boy.

"How did they like *Alice* over at the mill?"

Chris choked up and almost cried. "They called her a hearse. Said paint her black and hire a horse."

"They must have liked the fish."

"Said to leave it on the step and maybe a gull would fly away with it and me, too. And Ed up at the store called her a shit cart."

"Well, wipe your nose and listen to me. Whenever anyone does something new, especially if it's good and useful, there are plenty of people who will call you a fool for wasting time and material and think up foolish jokes to hurt your feelings and make themselves look good. You know this happens. When we decided to start this town, the Scarborough people called us looney. You can't argue with these people. All you can do is walk away." Ian looked over Chris's head, far beyond the east bank of the Machias River.

"But there may come a time when you will have to fight, when you can't walk away and still live in your own skin with yourself."

Chris sensed his father's serious tone, felt with a rush of pride that Ian was not talking down to a boy. He was a man talking to another man, and Chris was that man.

"When your family, your clan, your country really needs you, you have to step up, whatever it costs. I haven't yet had to do this, but the time may come. My father was the head of our family." Ian looked far away in his mind to the misty hills of Scotland. "Like our clan, and most of the Highland clans, we had given our word to follow Bonnie Prince Charlie—Prince Charles Edward—in his campaign to invade England, take London, and put his father, the rightful king, on the throne. The Highland clans gathered and, led by the Prince, invaded England successfully at first; but they were disappointed that they were not joined by the throngs of Englishmen they thought would rise to support them. The English drove the Scots back and many of their fair-weather friends deserted. They made a stand at Culloden, outnumbered, exhausted, and dismayed by failure and their long retreat; yet they stood by their word and boldly charged the English line. The English, who were well armed, well led, well rested, and well fed, over-whelmed the Scots, murdered survivors, killed cattle, burned shielings and houses and whole villages. Father never came home, but we knew he had stood by his word and done what he had to do.

Chris saw the whole scene in his head, felt the stubborn loyalty of the man who keeps his word. "Now I know what you mean, Pa, when you say there were worse losses at Culloden."

For father and son the misty hills of Scotland faded into the foggy banks of the Machias River. "You may come to better understand that later, Chris," said Ian. "But for now, walk away from it if you can, but always be the man you want to be. And sometimes you may have to fight for that."

Chapter 7

Boy

Ike and Si, just back from a voyage to the westward on *Polly*, sat across from each other at one end of a long plank table at The Wildcat Inn, two mugs between them, talking about their recent trip.

"That was a hard old trip down from Camden," said Ike. "Thick fog and light airs all the way."

"Yes, and a boy we should have left home. He knows bow from stern all right, but only guesses at port and starboard," said Si. "A chart to him is a mystery. No wonder. He can't read. And he can't count, either. When he gets to five knots on the log line, he is lost. And he was seasick from Vinalhaven to the mouth of the river."

"Well, he's big and strong and he can sure pull an anchor, and he can load firewood a cord at a time."

"I hear tell he wants to work in the woods. He can do that fine." There was a sarcastic edge in Si's tone.

"I'd give him a job on a logging crew, but what would we do for a boy? How about Big Dan? He's a bit young, but he's big and strong."

"He's big and strong, but he's not really a sharp tool."

"Sam Weatherbee?"

"Good God, no!" exploded Si. "I couldn't live with him two days. He's a chatterbox and he's fat and lazy unless you're on his back all the time."

"How about Robbie MacDonald? There's a good stout lad and smart, too," suggested Ike.

"Talk about smart! Take his brother, Chris, my little smelt—no, he ain't so little anymore. He's quick as a squirrel and real smart. He helped Steve Jones at the store for a spell and Steve said he was the best boy he ever had, except he couldn't reach the high shelves."

"He's only fifteen, Si, and not that strong."

"He's growing like June corn, and I can still pull an anchor. Takes two anyway. Chris can learn. I can teach him piloting in one trip and he won't forget what he learns."

"Does he get seasick?"

"I don't believe. He goes fishing way down beyond Sheep Island in that boat he built."

"Think Ian'll let him go?"

"Let me go ask him," said Si impulsively.

"Well, go ahead. We'll take him one trip and see how he does. Can he cook?"

"As well as that ape we had. But all he has to do is boil water and make coffee."

"Go ask Ian right away, then, because we want to be off to the westward by Thursday. Beal will sure have a load for us and I have half a load here." Ike raised his mug. "Have another for luck?" Si emptied his mug, declined another, picked up his hat, and was out the door.

Si strode into the spar shop like a man with a mission. Knowing he wanted Ian, Jackie nodded toward the back door and continued chipping away with his adze. Si found Ian outside looking unhappily at a 30-foot spruce log with the bark on.

"Looks good and straight, Ian. Why the glum look?"

"No good, Si. When we get the sapwood off, she'll twist. See how the knots come? Prob'ly grew halfway up a mountain."

"I got some good news now, or a good idea anyway. How about taking Chris with me and Ike for boy on *Polly*? He's getting bigger and stronger every day with all this rowing and fishing, and I could teach him piloting and chart work. He could learn the ropes and could hand, reef, and steer in a week."

"I dunno, Si. He's only fifteen."

"Boys go to sea in the British Navy younger than that. It would be a good chance for him to get ahead of these tree-choppers."

"Well, let's go talk to Alice." They found Alice on the doorstep taking a breather.

"Si and Ike would like to sign on Chris as boy on *Polly*. What do you think?" asked Ian.

"Oh no, Ian! He's too young."

"He's growing while you watch him, and these are good men. They won't ask more of him than he can do and I know he'll do the best he can."

"I'll teach him compass and chart work," said Si. "That will put him ahead of the rest of the lads."

"I was hoping I could make a good sparmaker of him," Ian said a bit wistfully. "He has a good eye for the right curve in a straight stick and good hands to get the feel of it. And he can handle an adze and plane about as well as Jackie."

There followed a considerable pause. Alice was looking over the narrow strip of salt marsh and across the river to the sandy mud flat below the mill wharf. Chris's boat, *Alice*, lay at the edge of the water and Chris was close by, digging clams. He drove his clam hoe deep into the mud, pulled back and up on the handle, dumped a clod of mud into the hole he had dug before. He picked over the clod, tossed several clams into his basket, and dug in again, hurrying to keep ahead of the coming tide.

"You remember," said Alice, "the day you and he and Robbie went into the woods for the tree for Sam Maverick's sloop? Chris was very nervous up there. I said then that he was a water boy. He is almost the only boy in town who can swim. If he is a water boy, the more he learns the better."

"Why don't we ask him?" suggested Si.

They hailed Chris across the river. He sloshed his clam hod in the water to clean out the sand and headed for home.

"You folks aren't down to living on clams now, are you?" asked Si.

"Oh no," replied Ian, "He's digging for fish bait. He'll go down on the first of the ebb tomorrow and be back with twenty or so good cod and haddock. What cod we can't eat, we'll trade to Steve at the store or salt or pickle. The haddock we'll smoke. Finnan haddie we called it in the old country."

Chris came up the bank with a questioning look on his face.

"Chris, how would you like to go boy on *Polly* with me and Ike?" asked Si.

"You mean it, Si? Go all day?"

"And all night."

"And see all the different harbors and islands?"

"Yes, and the towns and cities and the big vessels that go to Cuba and France and England."

"Pa, can I go?"

"Go one trip and see how you like it."

"C'mon, then, Chris," said Si, getting on his feet. "Let's go see Ike and sign on."

"Don't be in such a hurry, Si," Ian called after them. "What's the wages for a handy boy?"

"I dunno. Whatever the last one got was twice what he was worth. But Ike will use him right with the education thrown in. "C'mon, Chris, we're burnin' daylight."

They found Ike in the mill, discussing the proper stowage of rum barrels: "bung up and bilge free."

"Hey, Cap, here's *Polly*'s new boy," shouted Si across the shed.

Ike assumed a serious mien. "Come with me, boy, away from all this noise." He led Chris into a small room and sat at a desk too well finished to have been made in Machias. Chris stood before him.

"Now, boy, what is your full name?"

"Christopher MacDonald, sir." Chris was duly impressed by the formality of the occasion.

"And what is your father's name?"

"Ian MacDonald," replied Chris without hesitation.

"Do you of your own free will wish to sign articles as boy aboard *Polly*, to obey the orders of Captain and duly constituted officers?"

"Never mind all that," broke in Si. "Show him where to sign if you think he has to."

"Can you cook, boy?" asked Ike.

"He can make coffee and boil beef. Get on with it, Ike."

"Can you write your name?" asked Ike.

"Oh yes," said Chris.

"Write it here."

Chris took the pen and signed.

"Now you are a member of our crew and I am sure you will do all you can to make each voyage a success."

"Yes, sir," said Chris.

"Let's go aboard and I'll show you the ropes," said Si. "Can you set us off aboard in *Alice*?"

Three days later, with a cargo of deals and staves, they cast off and started down the river. Alice and Ian waved from the wharf, proud that Chris had earned a place as a member of the crew, but not a little apprehensive, too. The ebb tide helped old *Polly* beat down the river and then down the bay. Captain Ike at the tiller called, "Ready about." Chris went to one jib sheet, Si to the other. Ike called "Hard a-lee!" As *Polly* swung to face the wind, jib, staysail, and mainsail rippled, flapped, and slatted according to their size. *Polly* swung by the wind's eye and Chris put his weight on the lee jib sheet, made it fast as Si had showed him, and coiled down the loose line. He felt confident and a little proud that he could do his share.

As they threaded their way through the islands, Si pointed out landmarks. "That bare one over there is Sheep Island. You can tell because the sheep have eaten the grass almost down to the bare ledge. Just south of it is Sheep Island Rock. You can see it breaking white just aft of the rigging. It usually breaks except on the very top of a moon tide."

"I know," said Chris. "There's good fishing just outside of it on the coming tide."

"And that's Pulpit Rock standing up like a parson just to the westward. Take a good look at it so you'll know it in the fog. And that big woody island with the white sand beach is

Roque Island. There's no beach like that anywhere 'round." Chris listened and looked attentively until Captain Ike called, "Ready about."

Two weeks later, Robbie came puffing into the kitchen about lunchtime after running all the way from the minister's house. *"Polly's* back! She's coming up the river now, but not very fast. I could see Chris and Si and Ike aboard. The tide is running hard so they'll be a while."

"Have your lunch now, Robbie, and tell me what you learned today," said Alice.

"I wrote the Greek alphabet again and said all the letters and then did the Latin forms and we translated a verse from *Acts*. I suppose if you want to go to a high school, you have to learn all that, but chopping trees isn't much fun and every time I go into Pa's shop, I do something wrong."

"Eat your lunch and keep your courage up. Chris will be in soon and he'll have a tale to tell."

Polly rounded to and anchored, for the tide was too low to go alongside the store wharf. Ed Larrabee came off in his bateau to bring the crew ashore. Chris was in the kitchen minutes later.

"What-kind-of-a-trip-did-you-have-where-did-you-go?" rattled Ian, and before Chris could answer, Alice jumped in, "Are-you-alright?-Did-they-give-you-enough-to-eat?" and then Robbie, "How's-tight-Ike-for-a-skipper?" The words of all three tumbled over each other and everyone laughed.

"Begin at the beginning," said Alice, "and tell us all about it."

"We beat down the river," began Chris, "and went out through the islands and ledges. Si knows where the deep water is and where you can go at high and low water. We went by

Sheep Island and Great Spruce Island and up Mooseabec Reach. It's like a river, but open at both ends and it's full of ledges. The tide runs hard through it and you better go with the tide.

"Beal's is a little wharf like the mill wharf with a mill behind it. There were some staves in bundles and deals on the wharf and Chester Beal came aboard. He is a big man with almost no hair. He and Ike went into the cabin and Si and I tied up the sails. The tide was coming all the time, so when the skipper and Chester came on deck, we towed alongside and she grounded out during the night. We ran the throat halyard to a wharf piling so she couldn't fall over.

"Say, did you know that the compass doesn't even point north? Si showed me that the North Star bears about north by east. That's because the Earth is like a big magnet and the compass points to some place in the Arctic, and it certainly won't point north if you leave a knife next to it. Want to hear me box the compass?—North, north-by-east, north-northeast, northeast-by-north, northeast—"

"That's fine, Chris. Let's eat and hear the rest of it later," suggested Ian.

But Chris couldn't wait. Robbie had shot a deer two days before and between bites of Johnny cake and venison stew Chris told of his first glimpse of the Mount Desert hills through the haze off Petit Manan.

"I couldn't believe there were hills that high, but Si said, 'Wait 'til you get closer.' They got higher all day as we crept along toward Schoodic. That is a high hill itself and looks like an anvil. We could see the houses in Prospect Harbor as we went by. Crossing Frenchman Bay, the hills got higher and greener."

Chris interrupted himself with a lunge at the Johnny cake. "I don't know why it's called Frenchman Bay. We didn't see any Frenchies and there aren't any there now," Chris rushed on. "It began to rain and it breezed up so we ran into a little cove on Cranberry Island and anchored. I cooked salt beef and tea for them. Ike said there was almost nobody on Cranberry Island, but we went ashore in the morning and found a good little town and John Stanley sold us some salt fish at what Ike said was a good price. There's a bad ledge just outside, almost covered at high water, but it always breaks. It's called Bunkers Ledge, after one of the fishermen."

"What about the mountains?" asked Robbie.

"We saw them the next morning. They go right out of the water. Over near Southwest Harbor it looks like some giant took an ax and chopped down between the mountains. It's deep water right up to the cliffs on both sides and a family named Somes lives in a tight little harbor at the head. He's a farmer and doesn't have much to trade, but he has some daughters." Chris, who had been talking three feet to the yard, paused for breath and refueling from the stew pot and bread pan.

"How is Ike for a skipper?" asked Ian.

"All right," said Chris. "Si is better, but Ike knows his way around the coast and he's a great trader ashore. 'Buy low and sell high,' he says, and he does it."

With dinner cleared away, Chris rushed on with the story of his cruise. "We went down to Burnt Coat. I don't know whose coat it was that got burned, but it says Burnt Coat on the chart. Si says it's from some French word. There were quite a lot of people down there and they have firewood and fish and a sawmill, but they use the boards themselves. It's a real good harbor with a back door out into open water."

"Were you ever scared?" asked Alice.

"Not really scared for long," said Chris. "Coming into the Isles of Shoals was pretty scary at first. We were reaching along to the s'uth'ard with a nice little easterly and Si had just seen the top of Appledore when a bank of fog came in. It was dark, almost black underneath and white on top with the sun. It came on fast with little wisps of fog and then it shut down tight. It was scary because I couldn't see anything at all and everywhere looked the same—even the sky and water were the same color and I could hardly tell even which way was up. But Ike stuck his head out the hatch. He wasn't scared and asked Si, 'You get a bearing on her 'fore it shut down?'

" 'South by west,' answered Si.

" 'Fine, O,' said Ike and ducked below again."

Chris had slowed down during his disorientation, but built up speed again. "I looked at the compass and saw Si was steering the course and the compass knew which way was north and I felt better. Ike told me to go forward and look and listen. I had seen fog before, of course, and knew how to do that, but there wasn't anything to see or hear. We just sailed along, carrying our own circle of water and sky with us.

" 'Don't you think we're being set to the west'ard, Si?' said Ike. 'I'd give her half a point to the east'ard.'

" 'It won't hurt her, Cap, and there's nothing out here to hit anyway. We'll hear the gulls on Duck Island when we get close. Here, Boy,' Ike called me. 'Come aft and take the tiller and steer south by west, half west,' and after a while he said he heard birds and told me to look and listen again, and if I saw or heard anything to turn around and say what it was. I heard the sea breaking on Appledore and then the rocks, and then the sea smoothed out and I saw a big shallop at anchor and then Ike came on deck and we anchored and I could see the loom of shore on both sides." Chris's words came tumbling out all over themselves as he told about coming safe to anchor.

"What kind of place is the Isles of Shoals?" asked Alice.

"I don't really know. We didn't go ashore. After supper it was black dark in the fog. We heard loud voices and shouting and then a bell and some singing. We heard oars in thole pins and a man in a boat like *Alice* came alongside and asked who we were, and Ike asked if we were anchored in a good place. The man said it was all right on a quiet night, but not much in a northwester. That night we had a shower and a northwester in the morning. We saw a fleet of sloops getting under way, two schooners and a brig alongside a wharf in the lee of Appledore loading salt fish in barrels. It breezed up more and more and our anchor began to drag. So we got underway with a double-reefed mainsail and ran out of there.

"What was the bell?" asked Alice.

"There was a church and a fort on the island to the south, but we didn't go ashore. Ike said it was a rough place and there were no traders there, just thieves." Chris drew breath and sagged in his chair.

"Do you want to go again?" asked Ian.

"Oh, yes," said Chris, almost too tired to answer.

Chapter 8

The Fight on the Wharf

On a sunny day in late February, when the snow lay mushy underfoot, Ike Jones leaned against the doorpost of his mill, contemplating the pile of 12-foot-long deals, rough, unseasoned timbers 2 1/2 inches think by 11 wide, fresh from the saw. As a spring-like breath smelling of mud and salt grass wafted up over the meadows, it occurred to Ike that neither the deals nor the sloop *Polly* were making any money where they were, but if the two were together in Boston at this time of year, when lumber was scarce, the deals would bring a very good price and the sloop could bring a profitable cargo back to Machias. If only the weather would stay moderate. Well, he thought, you have to take some chances in this business. He went along the shore to ask Si to come with him for mate and he asked Chris to come as boy, his usual crew. He found young Nat Libby on the wharf and got him to round up a crew of boys to help load. Meanwhile, Ike went home, picked up his sea bag, put on his captain's hat, and went aboard *Polly* to get ready. It was low water with a light northerly breeze. *Polly* lay grounded out on a bit of sandy bottom alongside the wharf. When the tide came, she would float, even with a full cargo, and be ready to go down the river on the ebb tide. Ike turned and saw eight boys sitting on the pile of deals.

"Now, boys, get those critters aboard and down the hatch

and Si and I will be below to stow them. Dan, you take the first plank with Chris." Dan was a burly eighteen-year-old and Ike had paired him with Chris so the bigger boy could help the smaller. He turned, walked down the plank from the wharf to *Polly*'s rail, and went below.

Dan laid his big hands on the first rough, knotty unseasoned timber. "Think you can hold up your end, Shrimpo?"

Chris resented being called Shrimpo, but he picked up his end and said nothing. It *was* heavy, about all he could handle, but with clenched jaw he stumped down the bank and over *Polly*'s rail, still below the level of the wharf.

"Good for another one, Shrimpo?" This time Chris took the forward end and had to hold back hard to keep from falling forward.

"Don't drag your feet, Shrimpo." Chris clamped his jaw hard.

"You don't have to eat a whole lot more of this mud," said his brother Robbie as they passed. Again Chris made no answer.

"You getting tired?, Shrimpo?" jibed John O'Brien.

"Want to go swing birches with the children?" shot in fat Sam Westbrook.

Nat Libby came back at Sam," Can you chin yourself with one hand?"

And so it went as the heavy timbers marched four-legged down the bank, across the wharf and into *Polly*'s hold. Chris was getting hotter over the persistent insults, but the job was almost done and, as a member of *Polly*'s crew, he knew it had to be done before high water so they would have a fair tide down the river.

The last deal slid over the hatch coaming and Ike came on

deck. "Sky's been greasing over fast, Cap, while you were below," said Chris, "and the wind has shifted to the s'uth'ard."

Ike looked aloft at the graying sky and down the river at the growing chop. "We'll have a smart, cold beat down the river. The sooner we get started the better. She's already afloat." He handed the tally board to Chris as if he were the only possible choice, and went back into the mill.

As soon as they started carrying bundles of shingles down to Si in the hold, the ragging started again.

"You're real sharp with numbers, Shrimpo. Think you can keep up with us?" jeered Dan.

"Well, I can count to ten without taking my shoes off."

"Shrimpo," returned Dan, who didn't get the point.

Si called from the hold, "Move those shingles, boys, NOW!" Already *Polly's* rail was above the level of the wharf. The tide was coming fast.

Even little Jack Woodin jeered, "Captain's pet," as he carried his bundle of shingles by Chris.

John O'Brien muttered, "Mud hen."

And Sam Weatherall said, "Sitting out this dance, too, dearie?"

But Nat Libby said, "You got friends, Chris." And Robbie and Alec Campbell passed sympathetically.

"Good for nothing but tally boy," said Dan, who had finally gotten Chris's point about the shoes.

The bundles of shingles were now coming down faster than Si could handle them, so the line bunched up and the game of "Slash Chris" built up. "He's dumb. How did he ever learn enough to be tally man?"

"I dunno. Hatched out of a barrel and doesn't know his own father!"

"He's a bastard! Shrimpo's a bastard," roared noisy Dan.

Chris had been holding himself in hard. This was one of the worst grillings he had ever taken. Usually he was on the water when they were in the woods, but this time he had to stay with them, for he was a member of *Polly's* crew. That last slash was too much, and Chris boiled over. He slammed down the tally board and went for Dan, fists flying.

Dan was bigger and stronger than Chris, and his long arms held Chris off. Everyone laughed. Then Robbie bored in to his brother's help and Nat waded in on Dan's other side. The melee became general with Alec and Jack entangled with the others. Sam hung back on the edge of the battle. After some rolling around on the wharf, there came an upheaval in the pile as Dan hove two assailants off his back. Sam stepped one step too far back and hit the water with a big splash. Everyone rushed to the edge of the wharf. Sam came to the surface with his mouth full of salt water, splashing desperately as if trying to climb out, choked, and went down again. They could see him under water, thrashing and splashing and drifting away with the first of the ebb tide.

"Get a rope," yelled someone.

Chris jumped off the wharf feet first, and in three strokes caught up with Sam. He reached down, couldn't quite reach Sam, and plunged head and shoulders under. He grabbed the slack of Sam's shirt, came to the surface, and hauled Sam's head out of the water. Nat tossed the rope toward Chris, but it didn't reach. He went down the ladder with it.

Si, out of shingles and hearing the commotion, came on deck. Seeing Chris in the water, he tossed the end of the main sheet to Chris, who had begun towing Sam back toward the ladder on the wharf. Nat, although no swimmer, stood chest deep in the water, caught the slack of the rope, and hauled both boys to the ladder. He caught a turn around Sam's shoulder and the crew on the wharf hauled Sam up. Ike came running down the bank.

"What happened?" asked Ike, picking up the tally board.

"Roll that cask over here," said Si. "Grab his feet, Ike, and lay him across it." Salt water poured out of Sam's nose and mouth.

"Is he drownded?" asked John.

"Naw," said Dan with an eighteen-year-old's assurance. "After they puke out the water in their stummick, they always come around." But Si seemed less confident.

"Stop rockin' him now, Ike, and just hold him still on top of the barrel." Si pressed down on Sam's chest, slowly and rhythmically. No more water came out of Sam's mouth. Si continued. Everyone watched. When Sam gasped, coughed, and started breathing, everyone else started breathing. Si sat Sam down against the cask.

"Ike, go up to the house and get that flask of good French brandy you got tucked away somewhere. A tot of that will set the boy on his feet again."

"Did you see how Shrimpo went into the river after Sammy?" said Nat. "That was—"

"Where's Chris now?" asked Si sharply. Dan looked over the edge of the wharf.

"He swam ashore. He's aboard the vessel now," said Nat quietly.

"He's a gritty boy. There's no one that I see here ready to go into that cold, rough river to pull out one who had just called him a bastard—which he is not. I saw the wreck that took his parents. He's a good seaman and a good shipmate. I'll hear no more of this 'shrimpo' talk or someone'll get a big ear."

Ike came down the wharf with a flask and hastily, with his mind on other things, administered a dose to Sam. "You boys jump to it and get the last of those shingles down the hatch. Batten down, Si. Where's Chris?" Looking around, he ordered loudly, "On deck, Chris." He jammed his captain's hat down over his eyes and strode aft. Before dark, *Polly* was reaching out by Black Head through a chilly thick night.

The next day the wind shifted and blew quite fresh from the southwest. They lay over in Prospect Harbor and Ike kept them busy lugging and loading firewood and barrels of salt fish. Ike and Si knocked off for lunch about noon.

"Where's Chris?" asked Si.

"I sent him up to Harry's fish house with the wheelbarrow for another load of salt cod. Say, what was that dust-up on the wharf just before we left?" asked Ike.

"At first it was just boys," said Si. "They were pickin' on Chris. You know how boys will. Just like chickens. Peck at the one that's different. Chris has always been small so they got to calling him 'shrimpo' and of course he didn't like it."

"But he couldn't fight the whole crowd. How'd it start?"

"After you left, the teasing got worse, kind of mean. I didn't get it all 'cause I was below stowing shingles, but I got a good deal through the hatch. Maybe they were sore because you gave Chris the tally board while they had to lug shingles. Anyway, there was a lot of shouting and a scuffle and a splash, then another splash. I came out of the hatch in a hurry and saw the two boys in the water."

"But why'd the boys go overboard?"

"Don't know. You'll have to ask Chris. He was there."

The squeaky wheel of the wheelbarrow announced

Chris's return. "Sit down and have a bite," said Ike. "What started that fight on the wharf?" he asked bluntly.

"I dunno," said Chris. "They were picking on me and I just got mad."

"Why didn't you just walk away?"

"I couldn't. You gave me the tally board and I had to keep account of our cargo. I stood it as long as I could."

"You did just right," said Ike firmly. "I picked up the tally board."

"I don't blame you," said Si. "There comes a time when . . ., what was it, Chris, that touched you off?"

"Sam said I was hatched out of a barrel—"

"So you were," interrupted Ike.

"—and said I was a bastard because I didn't know my own father. I've got a father, and a mother, too, as good as any of them." Chris half-choked on the bread in his mouth.

Ike reached for the cheese and slowly cut off a piece. "You sure gave those boys something to remember, Si. I heard that part of it."

"I didn't like seeing my little smelt get hurt," said Si. "But I won't call you that again, Chris. You've outgrown it."

Chapter 9

Last Trip of the Year

It was a lovely warm November day—Indian summer they called it. Ike's sloop *Polly* lay alongside his wharf, loaded to the hatches with sawed lumber. On deck, Ian and Jackie had just lashed a boom they had built for a sloop in Boston.

"Bit late in the year to be going to Boston, don't you think, Ike," said Ian.

"Maybe," answered Ike, "but with winter coming on, Boston is dying for lumber and we can get a good price. We'll load old *Polly* with salt beef, pork, flour, tea, and rum and be back before the full moon."

"It's a fair wind, and she can't sink, loaded to her back teeth with wood like she is," said Si. "We may have to pump half of Old Ocean through her, but we'll get her to Boston and back again with a barrel of rum for the store and a new pair of shoes for you, Alice."

"We're wasting a fair wind," said Ike. "Chris, get the stops off the mainsail and hoist away on the throat halyard."

Polly swept down the river and Machias Bay before the puffy northwester. All night she pressed on, sheets bar taut, rigging straining, rail awash before the urgent northerly, a wind with winter behind it. In the cold November light of the next day, the hills of Mt. Desert, Isle au Haut, then the Camden Hills swept by.

"This can't last, Ike," said Chris.

"Sure it will," put in Si, "Record trip to Boston, Chris. We'll be unloading at Perkins' wharf day after tomorrow. Why don't you take a kink o' sleep, Likely Ike and I can handle her."

"All right. But prob'ly this will come in sou'west. It won't hurt a bit if you let her off to the s'uth'ard before it does."

"I know it, you old barnacle. Now, get below and turn in."

Later that afternoon the brave northwester died and snapped around into the southwest. The main boom slammed across and the headsails backed.

"The little smelt was right," said Si, trimming the main sheet as flat as he could. "He said it would come sou'west."

"Always does," growled Ike at the tiller.

Si belayed the main sheet. "Better get that big jib in, Cap. It's no good hard on the wind. Drives her head off to leeward something wicked."

"Leave it, Si. It's a mighty pulling sail. We'll stand offshore on the starboard tack and get as far to the s'uth'ard as we can tonight and tomorrow get a long leg to the west'ard."

"Get to the west'ard right now," said Si. "That's where Boston is."

"We better stay outside Matinicus Rock. Lots of dirty ledges inside."

"Well, alright, Captain, but Chris can take us inside by the Green Islands and Metinic." grumbled Si.

"Ready about. Let go jib sheet," shouted Ike in his captain's voice.

"Aye aye, sir," replied Si, sarcastically, "and leave the big jib just where the hell it is."

Strapped down and going to windward, *Polly* was a slow coach. Her bluff bows hammered along, bucketing into the growing southwest chop. She could not head closer to the wind than south by east and every sea set her to leeward of that.

But she shoved and bullied her way along as night, rising in the east, turned the blue sea to gray and then black and the stars flickered on, one by one.

Chris woke, built a fire in the fireplace, fried pork and potatoes, then called Si and Ike to dinner while he took the tiller.

They tacked at dawn, made a long leg of it past Monhegan. Late in the afternoon *Polly* weathered Pemaquid Point, then Thrumcap, and they slipped gratefully into Townsend.

The next morning they woke to a hazy, milky-blue sky, dark on the horizon, and a rising southwest wind already slapping the halyards against the mast, swishing purposefully through the rigging. Captain Ike eyed the horizon doubtfully.

"Good breeze, Cap. Let's get going," said Si.

"Head wind. Going to breeze up and rain. Maybe we'll lay over and wait for a chance along."

"*Polly's* got two sides and she can sail on both of 'em. You wait for a chance along and you'll ground on your beef bones. Let's go."

"No place to go," put in Chris. "Course to Boston is southwest by west, dead to wind'ard. With the breeze that's coming, there'll be a wicked sea off the Kennebec and this flat-chested old thing will never get to wind'rd. Until you get by Cape Small, there's no shelter better than here."

"Back to your blanket, Si," said Ike. "We'll lay over 'til the wind shifts."

Chris didn't mind a bit. He got Si to set him ashore and made his way between the fish flakes to Al's. With his foot on the step, the door popped open and a smiling Nomi welcomed him.

"Likely you're looking for Ruthie. She's in the back shed

washing clothes, but she'll be done soon. How's Jackie and your folks? You're looking good."

"Everybody's all right down east. We get along as best we can between supply boats. Clams and shore greens at the last of it."

"Well, set a bit. She'll soon be out." Chris sat on a bench by the window and wondered what Ruthie would look like. She would no longer be the shy little girl he had first met. On his occasional visits to Townsend, he had seen her grow into a girl of twelve and on successive visits gain figure and assurance. Then, through the kitchen door came a breathtaking young woman of fifteen. Their eyes met in mutual surprise, for she saw not a boy but a short, strong young seaman. "Oh, Chris, it's good to see you. What are you doing here?"

"Captain Ike decided to lay over a day. We're on our way to Boston in old *Polly*, loaded to the scuppers with sawed boards."

"Is Uncle Jackie with you?"

'No. He's home whacking down trees, making chips, and carpentering. What are you about?"

"I'm learning to read. I know my letters and can puzzle out words. Ma's teaching me."

"Out of here, you two," broke in Nomi. "Get over to the shore, Ruthie, and help your Pa with that load of fish he brought in last night." They found Al in the fish house.

He set Ruthie to washing the fish he had split and Chris to packing them in tubs between layers of salt with salt heaped over the top. Al questioned Chris about Machias, the voyage, and the situation in Boston, then turned again to splitting fish.

After a bit, two boys about fifteen looked in the open door.

"Hey, old squaw, who's your dirty-looking friend?" jeered

one. Chris took a quick step toward the door, still holding the big wet codfish he was salting, and with one full-arm swing splashed it across the side of the boy's head. The boy fell back, half rose between fight and flight. Chris drew back to strike again and the two fled.

"You don't have to take that, Ruthie, not while I'm around. I took it for a while—for too long—but no more."

"I wish you'd stay here, Chris. You could go fishing with Pa."

"I got a job with Captain Ike on *Polly*. We're on our way to Boston, loaded choking full of deals, with a boom lashed on deck. We ought to get a good price this time of year."

"When will you be back?"

"In a week or ten days, but if we have a fair wind . . .

"Hey, you two! I don't hear any fish being washed and I got this tub about full." The water splashed, the salt pile shrank, and the wide flat fish slapped into the tub. The washer and the salter felt comfortable with each other. So they did, too, over bread, tea, and pea soup at lunch and in the afternoon lugging wood and water with no further confrontation with Townsend boys.

During the afternoon, the blustery southerly wind slacked off and at sunset a shower came down over the hill. In the early dark of November, as they ate a fish chowder by the light of a candle, a foot on the step and a knock on the door announced the arrival of Captain Ike Jones.

"Better get back aboard, Chris," Ike said. "I found a few cords of firewood we can carry on deck. Firewood in Boston in November is money in your sock. This is going to blow itself out tonight and come off northwest, a fair wind for Boston and a bag of shillings."

"Northeast, more'n likely," said Al. "This time of year,

where the wind backed in, we could get quite a breeze."

"Godsend it's a fair wind and we'll ride it from Seguin to Cape Ann. Come on, Chris, the skiff's at the end of the wharf."

Chris thanked Nomi for the lunch and dinner.

"No trouble," said Al. "Glad to have your help. You do good work. Come again." Ike was already on the step. Chris shut the door on the table, the chowder, the warm fire, and said goodbye to Ruthie with his eyes. Ike picked his way ahead in the dark between the fish tubs, gathered up the painter, and climbed down the ladder, fumbling for the boat with his foot. On the edge of the wharf, Chris turned to back down the ladder. Ruthie materialized from the dark in front of him and held out her hands. He took them, drew her closer. Like two magnets, they came together. A hot wave flooded Chris from lips to toes. They held each other tightly, as neither had held anyone before. But only for a long breath. She pushed him off and was gone in the dark.

"C'mon down here, Chris. What have you, gone back for dessert?"

"Coming," said Chris, his foot on the top rung.

Chapter 10

The Boston Massacre (1770)

"Chris, what went on in this town last night?" asked Si as the crew of *Polly* sat on the edge of a Boston wharf. They had just finished stowing a cargo of salt beef, salt pork, flour, and rum in barrels and were eating a lunch and drawing a breath before sailing for Machias. "Lots of shouting about lobster backs, beating of drums, and a few musket shots. I know this town is all stirred up about the soldiers, but this must have been something special."

"It was some scrap," put in Chris. "I came out of The Open Gate on King Street and I was in the middle of a hot snowball fight. Seems though everyone was fighting the sentry in front of the Custom House and there was more than snow in some of them snowballs. They were yelling and cussing the sentry, but no one got close enough to hit him. Then some bigger men joined the crowd. One was a huge black man. I never saw one bigger. He walked right up to that sentry—I was close enough to hear him—and said right in his face, 'I'll have a claw off that lobster tonight.' The sentry was kind of scared by this and he was pretty well surrounded by people yelling at him and he called for help. An officer came out and a few soldiers with muskets, and a mob of people came running into the street from somewhere. The soldiers were all lined up and there were only a few of them, and the people behind me kept pushing forward so I couldn't get out. The black man said some more about lobster claws and swung a stick of cordwood at the soldier and knocked him flat and his musket went flying. They scrambled for it and the soldier got it. Everyone else was pushing and shoving and yelling and throwing things. I was trying to get out but I couldn't move. I heard someone shout 'Load,' and I guess they did, for all at once everyone shut up and I heard the ramrods rattle. Then everyone started shouting again and I was trying to get out of there and so were a lot of others. Someone shouted 'They're massacring the people' and someone else yelled 'Kill the lobsterbacks.' Then the officer shouted 'Present,' and you could hear it all over the street. Someone else yelled, 'Fire and be damned to you' and they did. The big black man was the first to get it but there was more shooting and more people hurt and I got out of there as fast as I could."

"What was that all about?" asked Si. "Just a few boys up to devilment?"

"I think they wanted to pick a fight," said Ike. "There's a pack of hellions in this town want to get the soldiers out of here and a good fight could be a way to do it."

"Well . . . " said Si. "They didn't have to kill a man to do it."

"I think he got just what he asked for," said Chris. "He told the sentry on duty he'd have a claw off him and knocked him flat with a big stick of cordwood. I'm not cryin' any for him."

"Still," said Si. "It is a bit rough on Boston to dump two regiments of soldiers on them, armed with muskets and bayonets and with no proper barracks and nothing much to do."

"Look, Si" said Ike with some emphasis, "Everyone in this

town, Whig or Tory, soldier, sailor, or tradesman, needs to eat and keep warm and will pay for deals, boards, shingles, and salt codfish. Our business has nothing to do with Liberty Trees or corruption of the customs officers. We are here to make money as fast as they can cut trees in Machias. Now get sail on this hooker and let's go east."

Chapter 11

Storm

They had most of the firewood loaded by noon and lashed down on deck, but then another wagon creaked down the wharf and Ike took another half-cord aboard at a very good price. As they tied a reef in the mainsail to raise it over the high deck load, the farmer called back,

"You goin' tonight, Cap? You might be glad of that reef. Goin' to blow some off shore."

"Nothing we can't handle in this stout little hooker," replied Ike.

By two o'clock they were underway before a fair northeast breeze that sent dark puffs down the sheltered water. As *Polly* waddled down the harbor, Si and Chris finished lashing the new deck load.

"Jeesly big deck load for this time of year," muttered Si on the lee side of the load. It may not all get to Perkins' wharf."

"Ike paid for it," said Chris. "He'll hang on to it long's he can. It's a fair wind and she ought to make it."

"If it don't get too rough."

The horizon ahead was clear and sharp under a high overcast. Chris boiled up a lunch of bread, beef, and coffee as *Polly* passed The Cuckolds at the entrance of Townsend harbor and bore off for Cape Ann, ninety miles away. Si took a watch below. Chris took the tiller. Captain Ike stood behind him looking at the compass.

"Course southwest by west for Cape Ann." Chris knew it perfectly well and Ike knew he knew it. Nevertheless, he was pleased to hear Chris repeat it.

"Southwest by west."

Ike stood comfortably in the hatch. *Polly*, with the wind on her port quarter, waddled happily along toward Boston.

The wind built up as it worked a bit easterly, raising a chop on top of a long roll.

"Cap, if you'll take her a while, I'll take up the lashings on that deck load," said Chris. "I hear them squeaking and talking." Ike took the tiller and Chris worked along the lee side, taking up what slack he could get on each lashing.

The high hump of Seguin passed to leeward and *Polly* headed for an empty horizon before the building northeast wind. The seas hove up *Polly's* broad stern, gave her a fine shove toward Boston, and rolled away under her lee bow in a smother of foam.

As the early dusk faded, the islands of Casco Bay dropped away under her starboard quarter. Si came on deck, paused in the hatch to look out over the darkened sea, the tumbled waves, the taut canvas, to feel the wind and *Polly's* hurrying pace.

"Breezed up some, ain't it, Chris? See the old bucket go. We're well on our way. Where are we, anyway?"

"Halfway Rock is off to starboard, about west-northwest and Cape Elizabeth is about there." He pointed ahead to starboard.

"I'll get a mug up and take a kink," said Ike. "Keep her going, boys."

"Can't do much else, can we, Chris?"

An hour later, even in the dark, they saw a heavy, dark

bank of clouds rise in the south and move rapidly up against the wind. A brief rain squall shut down and brought the wind more easterly.

"Time to put another reef in that mainsail," said Si.

"Past time," said Chris, bracing his feet and hauling hard up on the tiller as *Polly* tobogganed down a sea and took a big drink over her bow. "Come on up here, Ike, and give us a hand."

Ike pulled his jacket across his throat and his captain's hat hard down on his head. "I'll take her, boys, while you take a tuck in that mainsail." Si worked his way forward, slacked off the halyards and passed the tack earring. Ike luffed. Chris trimmed in the main sheet and, with *Polly* tossing wildly, bowsed down the clew earring already rove off; then worked forward tying in reef points while Si worked aft over the deck load. The two then swayed up the halyards again and Ike bore off before the wind. The reef eased *Polly* some until half an hour later the wind increased in another sharp rain squall with a few flakes of snow in it.

It was no night to cook. They chewed on hard bread whether they liked it or not, moistened with rain and salt water. Both wind and sea grew. In the dark, the wave crests showed a mean white.

"We ought to get in out of this," said Ike. "We'll run in for Falmouth. What's the course, Chris?"

"Prob'ly about northwest-by-west, but . . ."

Si broke in, "Running in on a lee shore in the dark and rain? We're doing all right now. We'll be up to Cape Ann by first light and Chris can take us in to Boston."

"I can take us into Boston," said Ike, sharply. "We'll hang on as we are."

They did. One big sea after another, driven by the increasing wind, reared up over *Polly*'s port quarter, its dirty-white top blown ahead of it. *Polly* hove up her broad stern, the cold salt top of the wave washed across her deck, over Si's boots. She lifted heavily, weighed down by her heavy cargo, and sank into the trough, the next wave already moving steadily up on her before she was ready. Again she was struck, lifted, rushed ahead, and then rushed again without a chance to draw breath. She was tired. The pace was too much. But still she kept on.

As the gale grew, the squalls came more frequently and colder, the seas came higher, driving faster, hitting harder. Her crew, cold and wet through their heavy woolen coats, with numb hands and feet, fought the tiller to keep *Polly* before the wind. The binnacle light had long since blown out. The man at the tiller steered by the wind, struggling to keep it behind his left ear.

Once Ike tried to heave to, seizing a moment when a less determined sea loomed up astern. With Chris and Si on the main sheet, Ike swung *Polly* toward the wind. She surfed heavily down the face of the sea, swung into the trough, and could not rise in time to face the next foaming crest. It charged over the rail, struck heavily against the deck load, and laid *Polly* far over. The weight of the rushing water dragged Ike from the tiller. Chris grabbed it, hauled it to windward, and Si let the main sheet run. The next sea was easier. *Polly*, off before the wind again, struggled to her feet. Ike crawled back up the slanting deck, his captain's hat gone, his weedy hair over his eyes, holding his hand to the side of his head.

"Nothing for it but to run for it now," shouted Si. They ran for it, shivering in the cold wind.

Sitting on deck, hanging to the taffrail with his feet wedged against the main sheet block, Chris pictured the chart of the Gulf of Maine in his mind's eye. The course from Boothbay to Cape Ann was southwest-by-west. He had sailed it before and knew it for a good course. It carried them safely outside the Isles of Shoals and the breaker off Boon Island. But this gale on the port quarter and these powerful seas were driving *Polly* to the westward, every one pushing her in toward that shelterless lee shore. Even if they passed clear of the Isles of Shoals, they would surely be set into the sandy bight north of Cape Ann; and with this sea running and this gale of wind, *Polly* could never beat out of that. So, thought Chris, bring the wind more abeam and keep out to the eastward. Probably in this gale *Polly* would never stand up to it, but it surely was worth a try.

"Your turn, Chris," said Si through his shivers, and Chris took the tiller. Every time *Polly* swooshed down the face of a sea, Chris eased her to the eastward, but as she rose heavily to the next, the top of it smashed into the deck load and she rolled dangerously to leeward. He had no idea of the time, but he guessed they had been gone from the Cuckolds almost all night, say almost twelve hours. They had been making six knots at first, but after they took the second reef and had begun surfing and turning sideways, they had been more or less drifting. Since trying to heave to, they hadn't done much. If they made rocky Cape Ann or the unforgiving beach inside of it before daylight . . .

Si was pumping. Maybe it would do some good. Surely this shaking up must have loosened her up some. Six inches of water sloshed about on the cabin floor. She couldn't sink, but she couldn't sail either, swimming about half under water.

The gale blew on and blew on. Pushed, urged, driven, lashed on by the wind, one after another the seas charged, each coming not hastily but deliberately, its ragged top shredded by the wind. *Polly* was beaten down, held down, unable to defend herself. She drove half submerged before the gale. Ike clung to the tiller. Chris crouched in the lee of the hatch. Si pumped. The rain stung and carried more snowflakes.

"Never mind pumping now," shouted Ike. "Get that jib off her."

"It's all that's keeping her before the wind," shouted Si between strokes.

"Take it in. It's too much for her." Si left the pump and crawled forward, found the halyard, slacked it off. The jib sagged down the stay, gave one big booming flap, split from luff to leach, and flew to rags. The next sea picked up *Polly's* stern. She swung to port, broadside to the crest. The rotten old mainsail tore right across from foot to throat, and *Polly* lay there, masthead in the water. The top of almost every sea washed across the deck.

Ike, dazed by his previous crack on the head and by the sudden and complete knockdown, clung to the tiller, not steering, just holding on.

"Where's Si?" shouted Chris. Ike was too dazed to do anything but hang on. "Si," shouted Chris into the gale. "Hey, Si! Where are you?" No answer. Chris listened through the roar of the wind and the tearing sound of breaking waves and rushing water. No answer. Si was gone, vanished, blown away in the windy dark.

Chris made his way forward along the deck load, cutting each lashing as he went. The pile of cordwood disappeared— gone. Tired old *Polly*, her belly full of lumber, filled to the gullet with salt water, lay broadside to the seas, adrift.

Slowly, dawn soaked through the night. Chris, very cold and a bit dazed, began to think again. The wind had eased a bit and the seas were not showing their teeth as savagely as before. It was cold. *Where are we?* thought Chris. *We could not have drifted far since we got knocked down. We must be still north of Cape Ann and got set into Ipswich Bay. We got to get out of here! But how?*

He realized he was desperately thirsty. He found the water jug afloat in the cabin, drank a pint without taking breath, and steadied the jug for Ike, still hanging to the tiller.

"What do we do now?" asked Chris.

"Steer southwest-by-west," mumbled Ike muzzily, fingering a lump the size of a muffin on the side of his head. Ike was going to be no help for a while, and that course was disaster. It was now light enough to see the compass and the wind had backed northerly as it eased. Chris cut away the foot of the blown-out mainsail, horsed down the gaff and cut the head of the sail clear. Relieved of the weight of gaff and most of the sodden sail, *Polly* struggled to her feet again. By hoisting what was left of the mainsail as a trysail, he could just get *Polly* underway and found he could steer east-southeast, maybe enough to clear Cape Ann.

Then a snow squall shut down and the wind backed even more northerly. With the help of another big drink of water and a piece of hard tack, Ike came to enough to steer east. With his fist and his face full of hard tack, Chris applied himself to the pump. He remembered with a jolt that the last hand on that pump handle had been Si's and felt an emptiness deeper than hunger. An important piece of him had drowned in the wet and windy dark. He did not stop pumping.

As the squall blew off to the eastward and as the snow

thinned, off to starboard loomed land, familiar land. Chris knew it for Cape Ann, safely to windward. Chris glanced at the compass.

"Now steer west-by-south, Ike, and we'll get into Gloucester."

Late that day, relieved of her deck load and the water within, and under her rag of a jury-rigged mainsail, *Polly* made her way at last into the shelter of Gloucester harbor, towed at the last by strong arms and helpful hands. As the anchor hit the mud, both men dropped dead asleep.

They awoke in the afternoon, had a meal and began to put things together. Ike went ashore to dicker for a new mainsail and jib. Chris cut away the jury-rigged mainsail and tightened up the standing rigging, badly stretched by the gale. At every turn he heard Si's voice. He knew Si would never come back, knew there was nothing whatever anyone could do about it, yet kept hearing "little smelt," "let's get on with it, we're burning daylight," and "He's a good seaman and a good shipmate."

Ike came aboard in the dusk to say he had found a second-hand mainsail that would do with a little sewing and an old jib. It was too big for *Polly*, but could be recut. The owners would trade for firewood, of which much was stowed below.

Chris thought of what Si would say to such "patch upon patch" repairs and choked up. Ike had not mentioned Si since the knockdown, but he had been thinking of Si all day and had come to realize that taking in the jib in the gale had let *Polly* broach to and be knocked down by the next sea. He knew enough not to dwell on his guilt and loss, but to cover them up with preoccupation with sails and firewood. But Chris's grief broke him down and his sympathy with Chris—who had never lost anyone close to him—came out. After a silence, he said, "We miss Si, don't we."

Chris nodded.

"He was real good to you, wasn't he."

Chris nodded again.

"Do you think he's happy in heaven?"

"I guess," said Chris, "but he isn't here."

"We can be glad we knew him and be glad he's happy now and that's the best we can do."

"I'll never forget him."

'Neither will I," said Ike. And they went to sleep in their damp blankets.

The next day, warm and sunny, they went alongside a wharf and spent much of the day unloading firewood. A boy with a wheelbarrow brought down the mainsail and began taking back firewood, of which Ike had Chris keep careful count. They spread the sail out on the wharf and, with palm and needle, went to sewing up loose roping and started seams. After both had sewed in silence quite a while, Ike asked, "How did you know what course to steer to get us out by Cape Ann? I told you to steer southwest-by-west, which is the right course to Cape Ann."

"You were, kind of muzzy, and I knew we had been pushed to the west all night by the wind and sea, so I guessed at it."

"Did you look at the chart?"

"I have a chart in my head."

They sewed on in silence. Chris moved on to a piece of loose roping, copying the same stitch as the original sailmaker had used. Ike watched Chris, who was intent on his work. He saw a well-built, clean young man, short for his age, but tough and wiry. *It must have been quite a feat to cut away the blown-out mainsail and to rig a trysail that cold and windy night,* Ike thought. *He certainly has profited by his two years as boy under Si's guidance. He's young and he should come cheap.*

"Chris, what am I going to do for a mate?"

"Dunno."

"Do you want to try it?"

"Aye, aye, sir." And thus Chris became mate of *Polly.*

Chapter 12

Ruthie

Chris was helping Ian in the spar shop between trips to Boston in *Polly*. He and Jackie were fitting jaws to a new fore gaff for a schooner in Prospect Harbor. It was an intricate job for hatchet, plane, and draw knife. Jackie had selected a twisty piece of oak and had fashioned two jaws to follow the grain. He and Chris were smoothing up the rough edges.

"You been in Townsend lately?" asked Jackie.

"Not since that storm when Si was lost," answered Chris with a catch in his throat.

"How was my sister getting on, and Ruthie?"

"I didn't get much chance to visit. You know Cap'n Ike. Always in a hurry to load another thousand feet or a barrel of rum. I did see Ruthie for a bit. She said fishing was good. Al had the flakes full of cod drying and a couple of barrels of salt cod to put aboard *Polly*." He did not mention that he and Ruthie had shared a sense of the community's coolness, not to say rejection. They had also shared a sense of acceptance of one another.

Ian came into the shop to inspect the work. "Looks good, boys. Jackie, be sure to show Chris how to work in the curve where the jaws turn up. It's 'most dinner time, so come in when you find a good place to stop. Chris, take a look at that sloop coming up the river. Maybe you've seen her someplace before."

Chris looked past Ian as he stood in the door. "She looks like that sloop fishes out of Townsend. B'longs to a fella named McCobb. Looks like he's anchoring but not staying long, leaving his mainsail standing."

"There's two women coming out of the cabin," exclaimed Ian.

Alice burst out of the kitchen door. "Two women! What two women?" She looked, wiped her eyes with her apron and looked again. "That's Nomi and her daughter. They're coming ashore."

All four rushed down to the shore, Alice flapping her apron, the others waving. The skiff grounded on the sand and was pulled up high and dry with a rush.

"Nomi, What's happened? What brings you here?" The sad look of both women damped the pleasure of meeting. Nomi stepped out of the skiff, almost fell against Jackie and sobbed, "Oh John, he's gone. Al's gone."

Ian spoke quietly to Steve McCobb, "What happened?"

"Al McKown was lost."

"How was that?"

"Went fishin' about ten days ago now and didn't come back. Came off a real hard squall. Northwest rain and hail and blowin' blue Jesus. First we all thought he'd been blown off shore and couldn't row back against it. Next day it shifted southwest, and the next morning Ed here found Al's boat all stove up on Punkin Rock. Nomi's all broke up, of course. Wanted to be with her own people. We knew her brother was down this way. We were making a run to Eastport anyway so brought her and her girl along."

Ruthie, teary too, held her mother's hand as she sobbed out the story to her brother. Chris listened and, as the story came out, took Ruthie's other hand.

"It's cold and wet out here," said Alice, Let's go up to the house. Steve and Ed, stay and have a lunch with us."

"No thanks, Alice," said McCobb. "We better take a fair tide down the river and maybe as far as Cross Island."

Steve and Ed shoved the skiff off and departed. The others made their way up between dripping blackberry bushes to the warm kitchen. They had a bowl of hot pea soup Alice had made of dried Navy-issue peas.

Nomi didn't eat much. Exhausted by grief and the voyage, and relieved at finding her brother, she went to sleep on Robbie's bed.

Ruthie sat next to Chris at the table and reached her hand down to Chris's, feeling for support. When everyone got up, she whispered, "Stay with me, Chris." Jackie and Ian headed back to the shop.

"Coming with us, Chris?"

"Go ahead. I'll be along."

When the dust settled, Chris asked, "How was it, Ruthie?"

"Awful. When he didn't come home the first night, we wondered and worried. There had been a hard storm in the afternoon and we kept telling each other he'll be home in the morning. He always takes a lunch with him and a bottle of water.

"The next morning I went over to the store and Steve was there and he said, 'Still blowing northwest. A hard pull against it. He'll likely be in this afternoon.'"

"Waiting is hard," said Chris.

"The wind shifted in the afternoon and blew on shore. We told each other he'd sure be in for dinner. We listened and listened. I went down to the shore to show a light. The wind blew harder, and it was cold and the light blew out and I was scared so I went home. We were not so much worried as afraid for him. We lay down and finally went to sleep for a little while.

"In the morning, I went back to the store, but no one knew anything, but they all tried to encourage me."

"You can tell when they do that," said Chris.

"About noon, Ed came in, looked at me, and pulled Steve into a corner. I couldn't hear what they said, but as they came out, Steve said, 'You got to tell her, and her mother, too.' So Ed told me he had found our boat wrecked on an island and no sign of Pa."

"I wish I had been there," said Chris.

"I really wish you had," Their hands were tightly tangled up in each other's.

"Ed walked me home and told Ma. She must have been expecting this for she just said, 'Thank you, Ed. He was a good man,' shut the door and flopped into a chair. She was too tired to cry and we hadn't had much to eat.

'I want to be with our own people,' she said at last. 'But our own people, those who are left, have gone to Canada and you and John were just babies when the Gilmores took you in,'

'Yes, I want to go to John,' she said. 'He's all I've got but you. Let's go to John.' She was all broke up dry crying and so tired she could hardly sit up.

"I went back to the store. Alec, the store man, asked, 'How's she taking it?'

'Hard,' I said. 'She wants to go to my Uncle John's.'

'He's down east somewhere. If he's still with Ian, he's prob'ly in Machias building spars.'

'How do I get to Machias?'

'Right now,' Alec said, 'Steve and Ed are putting the last barrels aboard Steve's sloop for a run to Eastport. Maybe you can catch them.' "

"Good news," said Chris.

"I ran for the shore, hair all adrift, pounded down the wharf and found Steve. 'Sure we'll take you if you'll come right away. Fair wind to the east'd.' I ran home, told Ma. She grabbed up her money bag and a blanket and we made it to the shore as Ed was hoisting the mains'l."

Ruthie collapsed against Chris' shoulder and he held her close.

"You certainly did a good job, Ruthie. Got your mother down here safe and sound where she wants to be."

"Me too," said Ruthie.

Nomi woke up much refreshed.

"I must look like a real wild Indian. Where can I wash up?" she asked.

She returned from the well with the empty wash basin and her hair all braided up as usual. "Al's gone," she said in a controlled tone. "I know he's not coming back. We talked about this before. I just have to go ahead as best I can. So what's next? We came down on you suddenly. Is there a bed we can find?"

They talked more about it when Ian, Jackie, and Chris came in from the shop. "There's Robbie's bed while he is in Cambridge studying to be a doctor," said Alice. "Chris can stretch out on the floor until *Polly* sails again. We can put up Nomi and Ruthie for a few days," she went on, "but where are they going to live?"

"I want to live with John. We need each other now."

"Yes," said John, "I'll make room for them."

"Can't do it," said Ian. "Too small. You couldn't build one more bunk in there, never mind two—and all their gear. We'll have to go back to Townsend and get that. No, what we'll do, Jackie and I, and Chris while he's here, we'll run up an ell on

Jackie's house and make a real nice place for them."

Jackie was reluctant to accept, but Nomi and Ruthie were all for it.

"I'll see Ike about the lumber tomorrow," said Chris, he paused, "he owes me."

Chapter 13

The Boston Tea Party

The main room of the Wildcat Inn was busy as usual on a Saturday afternoon in early March 1774. At one end was a brick fireplace in which a hot fire burned, open both into the kitchen and into the main room. The room had windows of oiled paper, which let in some light, and one glass window looking out onto the porch and across the river beyond. The ceiling was crossed by beams that still showed adze marks. Over the fireplace, the ceiling was darkened by smoke, but over the rest of the room it was just as it came from the mill. In front of three walls stood benches and in front of each, a long table. The room had a warm, comfortable smell of wood smoke, new wood, cooking, and tobacco smoke. There was a cheerful buzz of talk.

"Caleb saw a bear yestiddy. Must have just come out of his winter den. Scratchin' his back against a big spruce tree. No, he didn't have his gun and anyway, he'd be tough as a boot and skinny."

"Look, there's a coupla fellas rowing up the river. Wonder who they are and where they've been."

"Rowin' a little like Chris, but *Polly*'s not due back yet."

"Wonder what's doin' in Massachusetts. It's been kind of quiet there since last summer. This business may all blow over where they gave up a lot of the taxes and such."

"They've still got a tax on tea and Sam Adams is making a thing of that."

"They're really crackin' down on the customs officers. A few shillings won't buy you a stamp on Dutch tea any more. And there is still the tax on English tea."

"Sam Adams is stirring that pot, but it isn't a hot one. Dutch tea is better and cheaper if you go to the right shop, eh, Steve?" Laughter spread throughout the room, but Steve did not join in.

Steps were heard on the porch and Chris and Robbie came in.

"What brings you here?" asked Steve quickly. "*Polly* all right? You didn't lose her, did you?"

"No, Steve, your barrels of beef are all right. Here's the cargo list. We're anchored down by the Rim. The tide was running out hard and there was no wind. Ike and Nat will bring her up after low water in the morning. I thought Steve would like to know what's coming, and there's a lot coming."

Chris explained that Robbie had been in Cambridge studying to be a doctor with Dr. Peabody. "He has read a great deal in the doctor's medical books, and has listened and watched and assisted with his patients. And he has been out and around in Cambridge and Boston."

"The big news," said Robbie, "is that a gang of the Sons of Liberty and others dumped three shiploads of tea into Boston Harbor."

"Three *shiploads?*"

"Three shiploads."

"What'd they do that for?"

"Seems the East India Company had a lot of tea they couldn't sell at their price, so Parliament granted them a monopoly to sell it in America."

"What's a monopoly, Bub?"

"That means it's a crime for anyone to sell any tea at all in America except the East India Company. They sent three ships to Boston and appointed only a few consignees to sell it. Two of them are Governor Hutchinson's sons. They would have made a pretty penny."

"Your tea has the right stamp on it, don't it Steve." More laughter erupted around the room and, again, Steve did not join in.

"Sam Adams got all stirred up by this and stirred up a lot of other people too," Robbie continued. "If Parliament can grant a monopoly on tea, they can do it on cloth or boots or salt fish or anything, then tax it and ruin us all.

"At the end of November the *Dartmouth* came in loaded with tea. Sam Adams called a mass meeting in Fan'l Hall and thousands came. They called themselves The Body and voted to put a guard on the *Dartmouth*, and any other tea ships that came in, to be sure they didn't unload and told them to take their tea to hell back where they came from.

"But the governor wouldn't clear the ships to leave until they were unloaded. So Sam called another mass meeting, this time in Old South, and sent a messenger to the governor in Milton, asking for clearance. I couldn't get in, but standing at the door I heard all the speeches about British tyranny while they were waiting. When the messenger came back, there was a sudden silence while he delivered his message. Then Sam Adams announced in a loud, firm voice, 'There is nothing more this meeting can do for our country.'

"Then all hell broke loose. There were Indian war whoops and cries of 'On to Griffin's Wharf' and 'Boston Harbor for a teapot.' A crowd of men waving hatchets, who'd blacked their faces, and a lot of others, too, ran for the shore. I had a head start. When the blacked-up ones ran out on the wharf, they divided into three groups, one to each ship. They broke open the hatches and as fast as the boxes were passed on deck, those Indians smashed them open and dumped the tea overboard. Over a hundred thousand pounds worth of it."

The rafters of the Wildcat Inn seemed to ring with silence as the enormity of the deed percolated. Three shiploads of tea! Worth thousands and thousands of pounds! DESTROYED.

"Don't sound like Injuns to me," ventured one into the silence.

"It wasn't. I saw several people I had visited with Dr. Peabody when they were sick, and several doctors, too. And those Indians were all blacked up and ready to go,"

"Chris, what did you see?"

"Nothing. I was aboard *Polly* down the harbor the whole time."

"What do you think of it?"

"Since you asked me, I'll tell you. I think it was piracy, pure and simple, and a criminal waste of tea."

"Don't you think it's about time we Yankees did something about British oppression?"

"I'm not a Yankee and I haven't been oppressed. I work for Ike carrying cargoes and selling them. I have nothing to do with politics or tea or monopolies or whatever."

Another silence.

"Chris is right. Let's mind our own business. Mine is cutting wood."

Ben Foster, who had fought at Louisbourg, said, "Dumping the tea didn't solve anything. We are all wide open here. The Royal Navy could blockade the whole coast and then where would you sell your staves and shingles and where would Steve get his flour and salt beef and rum. You'd be down to clams and shore greens in a month. They could sail in here in a 12-pounder sloop of war and wreck our mills and everything we have built here. Have any of you faced the business end of a 12-pounder? Let the sleeping lion lie until he wakes up, and that may not take long."

"I for one, will fight for freedom!" cried someone. "Who's with me? Hurray, hurray for the Sons of Liber*tay*!" Many voices joined in the cheer.

"No tea for me. Red rum and liberty. Glenn, rum all round and a drink to Sam Adams and the Sons!"

The low rafters of the Wildcat Inn rang again with cheers for freedom from British chains and toasts to Sam Adams and the Boston Indians. The meeting adjourned to the shore, where the towering flames of a huge bonfire lit up the sky and the whole town.

Several of the more sober ones withdrew through the kitchen, muttering, "These fellas are crazy." Steve went up to his store with his musket, lest the idea of dumping tea suddenly proved attractive to the locals.

Chapter 14

Wedding

"Dance tonight," said Ian. "Better take your girl out among 'em for a change."

"We really should," said Ruthie. "If we make an effort, maybe some of them will respond."

"They should. You're quite a handsome woman, you know."

Before dark the windows of the Wildcat Inn were brighter than usual, for Glenn had a bright fire going and even a few candles for the party. They could hear Ed Larrabee's fiddle tuning up, an accordion, and two Jew's harps. Then the fiddle led off and the other instruments picked up the rhythm, if not the harmony. When Chris and Ruthie opened the door there was one circle of people going one way and another circle going the other, and Jerry O'Brien and Charity Libby going down the middle, swinging each couple as they came to it.

Several surprised faces turned toward the door, but the dance went on to its triumphant finish.

When the circle broke up, Nat and Foxy came over and spoke to Chris and Ruthie, and a lady on the chaperone bench smiled in a friendly way. But soon the orchestra started up again. There followed some confusion as people chose partners. Chris and Ruthie found themselves between Big Dan and

Agatha Jones. Agatha said softly, "Why don't you go over to the other side, next to Sam Weatherbee and Judith?" She dropped Chris's hand and gave him a little push. They crossed over, not noticing the dark looks from Sam. Judith let them in. "Circle right," called Red.

"Skip to my Lou." The orchestra picked it up and around they went.

Then all into the middle and out.

"Swing your partners."

Sam reached across in front of Ruthie and Chris and swung Judith.

"Circle left."

Sam clung to Judith's hand and circled off to the left, leaving Chris and Ruthie outside the circle and looking at the backs of the dancers.

Ruthie got the message first and it didn't take a mocking glance from Agatha across the room for Chris to catch on.

"This is not our party'" said Ruth. "Come on, Chris." They slipped out the door as the dance ended, so they didn't see the lady on the bench rise up, cut Sam out of the crowd into the kitchen and slap him hard on the face three times. Right, left, right.

"Don't you ever do a thing like that again, Sam."

"We didn't mean nothin' by it. We was just funnin'."

"It was a mean thing to do to anyone, 'specially a stranger and most 'specially to the man who pulled you out of the river last year. Now you get right out there and apologize."

"He's already left," grumbled Sam, "and I don't apologize to a dirty black—"

"Then go home. I won't have you show your face in here tonight."

Outside in the cold dark, Ruthie cried. She was hurt, insulted, rejected by the community. So was Chris. His impulse was to go back in and leave a mark on Sam Weatherbee he would never forget. Yet that would break up the party and degenerate into a dusty scuffle with Chris on the bottom of the pile. No, he decided, this was one more "walk-away" situation, much as he knew Sam needed a black eye.

He tried to comfort Ruthie, took her home, hugged her close and failed utterly in making her feel better. He left her to her mother.

Chris found Ian and Alice by the kitchen fire and told them the story. Ian was angry. "I'd have given that Sam two black eyes on the spot. I may not wait until tomorrow. No one treats my boy and his girl that way." Ian was putting on his jacket.

"Sit down, Pa. I'll skin my own skunks," said Chris.

"What are ye about to do, laddie?"

"I'm going to go to sea. I can do anything any able seaman can do; hand, reef, and steer, knotting and splicing. I can read a chart, lay a course, take bearings. I know the coast from Eastport to New York in fog, snow, or night, and I don't need to take any trash from that kid or anyone else."

"Sleep on it, boy," said Alice. "There's people to consider besides yourself."

"Tell me just what happened at the dance, Chris. Who did or said what? Who needs a black eye and why?" asked Ian.

So Chris went over the whole incident. Spread out in detail, and considering the infantile sense of humor of Sam and Judith, it began to look more like a silly prank than a calculated insult and rejection. After consideration and reconsideration, Chris decided again that this was a "walk-away" situation—it was unkind and mischievous, but not worth fighting for.

He slept on it. When he awoke, his first thought was of Ruthie, discouraged, rejected, abandoned. He knew Ike would want to sail on the morning tide and he also knew he could not leave Ruthie thus. He must see her right away.

Chris knocked on the door of the ell to try again to console Ruthie, but Jackie said that Steve's boy had told her she was wanted in the store and she'd left.

In the store he found her in the back shop, bent over the molasses barrel drawing a quart for Mrs. Sullivan. He started to explain to her back. "Ruthie, I . . ."

She was startled, turned, spilled some molasses. "Oh, it's you."

"I want to talk to you about last night."

"I don't want to think about last night, or hear about it, and I'm going to stay with Ma and Uncle John and work at the store and be a drag on no one."

She stood up, slopped a dollop out of the quart measure, licked it off her hand, and with determined step, strode back up to the counter. With a steady hand she poured a quart of molasses into Mrs. Sullivan's jug labeled "Vinegar." The store suddenly resembled an ant's nest. Mrs. Sullivan, a long, lean lady with a short fuse, was demanding half a gallon of vinegar, a quart of molasses, and for Ruth to wash out the jug. Ruth said she was sorry and broke down crying, which did no good. Steve wanted to know what had happened and to whom. Two unregenerate woodsmen were still laughing immoderately when the door was slammed open by Ike's new boy, Nat.

"Chris, come along. Hurry up. We're sailing on this tide and Ike is boiling over. Get moving."

Chris wanted desperately to talk to Ruthie. He couldn't leave her smudged with tears and molasses. He broke through

Mrs. Sullivan's outrage, Steve's harangue on the cost of molasses and vinegar, turned Ruthie's back to the counter, and gently wiped off her face.

"Ruthie, dear," he said, deeply sincere, "I have to go. Old Ike-in-a-hurry is yanking on my halter. Be strong till I get back." And right in front of the whole store he kissed her, squeezed her hand, and left with Nat.

It was a short cruise. They left Machias only half loaded, for Ike planned to pick up cargo at various harbors along the shore, and by mid-April the season was getting on.

At Cape Split they got a few cords of firewood. At Prospect Harbor they found little, but saw a large crew was very busy unloading a topsail schooner, putting her cargo aboard wagons and concealing it behind boards. Ike enquired about the cargo and got no answers, but Chris noticed a small keg such as is used for gunpowder. The pile under a tarp in the middle of each wagon could have been muskets and the wagons were heavily loaded. The curious were not warmly welcomed and Ike soon left.

At Herring Gut their reception was cool, but at Boothbay they found several thousand feet of sawn boards and were advised to stop at Falmouth.

Captain Mowatt of a British armed schooner had seized and condemned several hundred feet of boards, which had not been cleared by the Supervisor of the King's Woods. Mowatt wanted Ike to take them to Boston, but Ike refused.

"That pot of pitch is too hot, Chris. If we put our hands into that, we'll get burned and the pitch will stick to us a long time."

As they were loading for the return trip, Chris smiled as he ran his hands over a molasses barrel consigned to Steve Jones.

With the fair winds of early May, the warm weather, and the long days, they were back in Machias River in a week, even with a stop at Boothbay. As they came up the river, Chris looked eagerly for the white flash of Ruthie's apron on the shore, but he looked in vain.

Nomi opened the door to Chris's knock. "Oh, Chris, I'm so glad you are back. She's been watching the river on every flood tide since the day after you left. She's over at your house reading with Alice."

Chris found her trying to deal with Christian's fight with Apollyon in *Pilgrim's Progress*. However, her interest in a flesh-and-blood Christopher was much stronger than anything literary. Alice welcomed him but Ruthie just stood there and dug her shoulders into his armpit.

"Nice day out," said Chris. "Let's take a walk."

"Be back for dinner," Alice called to their vanishing backs.

They went down to the shore in the sunset, through the fields starred with red clover and buttercups. They sat on the log they now regarded as their personal property.

"I had to leave in such a hurry last time," said Chris, "I was too quick, but you looked so sad and upset and Mrs. Sullivan and Steve were yelling at you and Nat was dragging at the back of my shirt and your face was all smudged with molasses and I just did it."

"I am so glad you did."

"How have you been? Did Steve fire you?"

"No. He got me to wash out the jugs, though. I missed you something awful."

"How have people been to you? Do they still pull away?"

"Not so much. Ada Weatherbee was pleasant and Sam said 'Hello,' as if he was pushed and went away. Prudence Sullivan thanked me for a good job washing those miserable jugs and a few people tease me and ask if I'm selling kisses. Most people just buy what they want, say nothing, and go away. I'm not in the store very often, anyway, and I help Ma and Uncle John and Alice."

"It's much the same with me. I get on fine with Ike and Nat, but most other people sort of pretend they can't see me. When I was fishing, they would trade a chunk of venison for a fish but it was just a trade: 'You take this; I'll take that,' and not even a 'thanks' or 'good-bye'."

"We must take care of each other," she whispered.

She sat closer and dug her shoulder deeper into his armpit. He drew the arm behind her back and she leaned back into it. She felt secure, comforted, safe. Chris felt her strong back under his hand and then as he reached farther, her breast. They slipped back off the log into a nest of beach grass behind it and were overcome with love and the need to be very close to each other.

Deeply shaken, changed indeed, by the moving discovery that each was not alone in the world, but had a friend, an ally, a shipmate, they climbed the bank to Alice's supper.

During the next two days they sat often on the log and thought of the future together—its possibilities and impossibilities and long chances. Their mutual conclusion was that whatever the future brought, they could deal with it better together than apart and they had better get married and let the world know it.

The minister questioned them on the sincerity of their intentions, their relationships with God, whether Chris could support a family, and other matters both practical and spiritual, and at last agreed to marry them the following Sunday afternoon. It was a simple ceremony right out of the book. Alice, Ian, Nomi, and Jackie were present, and a few others who drifted in: Nat, Foxy, Steve, Prudence Sullivan, Jerry O'Brien. Chris missed Si very much and Ruthie her father, Al.

But the knot was tied. A toast was drunk and Ruthie became Ruth MacDonald. Whatever came, they were committed to deal with it together.

Chapter 15

The *Halifax*

On *Polly*'s first trip after the Port Act closed the port of Boston in June, Ike, Chris, and the new Boy, Nat, came by Cape Ann about dusk, and, with a fair southeasterly breeze and fog hanging aloft, slipped into Boston Harbor unseen. They landed their lumber at the government wharf. Over the next few nights, wagons brought down their return cargo and again they slipped by the patrols unseen. Chris was a little doubtful about breaking the law, but Ike said,

"The law is not our business. Everyone in Boston has to eat and keep warm and they'll pay for it."

But the second trip was not so easy. They made Cape Ann before dawn in a light, southeasterly air and choking thick fog. *Polly* glided silently over the easy swells. Chris listened for the distant sound of surf on the ledges. When Cape Ann was well astern, he bore off west-by-south for Boston. Daylight filtered through the fog.

"This little air will likely die out and come in sou'west as the sun rises," said Chris.

"How do you know?" asked Nat.

"Usually does," said Chris. "I been here before." *Polly* glided quietly on, carrying her little circle of gray sky and gray water with her.

Nat jerked alert and pointed to port. "Hear that, Chris?"

But Chris had heard it, too. Eight clear strokes of a ship's bell. Then a voice: "Lights are bright, sir."

"Relieve the wheel and lookout," said another voice. "Watch below lay below."

Chris said in a subdued tone, "That's a King's ship. None of us do that foolishness. Prob'ly nearly a mile away, though. Voices carry in the fog." He let *Polly* off to west. "Ease the main sheet a grind. We'll keep away from him if we can."

Apparently the King's ship was bound for Boston, too. They sailed along together on parallel courses, invisible to each other, the naval vessel gradually pulling ahead.

"Why not tack," asked Nat, "and go off to the s'uth'ard away from him?"

"Because," Chris replied. "The way this wind is working around to the south, he will have to tack pretty soon, and there we'll be, right under his lee. It's a gamble, Nat. We'll hang on a while. It's beginning to be day. Why don't you go below and get us a bite to eat if you can do it without disturbing Captain Ike." Nat went below and the two vessels sailed on, the naval vessel still drawing ahead slowly.

As the sun rose, the fog thinned and turned milky. To windward, a topsail schooner materialized, towing a small boat. Chris tacked at once, bore off with the wind on his quarter, and ran back into the fog. The schooner followed, but Chris hoped they would be hidden in time and called Nat on deck to trim the main sheet. He hauled up to about south-by-east, hoping to cross ahead of the schooner. The rattle of blocks and slatting of sails brought Ike on deck.

"Where are we? You should have called me."

"We're about two miles off Gloucester and heading to cross the bows of a British naval vessel. If we make it, we'll be clear away and out to sea in the fog."

"I'll take her," said Ike, pulling his captain's hat hard down. "Nat, go forward and look and listen. Chris, stand by sheets. What's your course?"

"Full and by. Hold her up to wind'ard as much as you can without pinching her."

"Teach your grandmother to suck eggs," grumbled Ike.

"We ought to make it. She's about over there." Chris pointed a little forward of the starboard beam.

They sailed on in tense silence, peering into the thinning fog, listening for the squeak of a block or the slat of a sail. The shadow of a shroud showed dimly against the mainsail.

"There she is," called Nat, pointing almost abeam to starboard. They all saw her at once, dimly through the thinning fog, about two hundred yards away and coming on fast.

"We're going to make it," said Chris, quietly, tensely. "Bear off a mite and give her a mouthful. It'll be close, but we'll make it." The long spear of the schooner's bowsprit was lunging at *Polly* and there was more than a ripple under the schooner's bow, but she drew aft and passed close astern. A voice from the schooner's quarterdeck shouted, "Heave to, damn you!" and a puff of smoke came from a forward gun port.

"He'll never catch us now," said Chris. "He's to leeward and astern."

But Ike rolled the wheel down and called to Nat to take in the jib and back the staysail. "We don't have to fight the Royal Navy, Chris. Take her while I go below a minute."

Without her jib and with staysail backed, *Polly* awaited the arrival of the boat the schooner had been towing, manned by a petty officer, a midshipman, and four oarsmen armed with cutlasses. The officer came up the starboard side accompanied by the young midshipman and two of the seamen. The officer addressed Ike.

"Thomas Sparke, sailing master of His Majesty's armed schooner *Halifax*. Your papers, sir." Ike handed him two documents. He read the worn parchment first. "That's all right. Regular ship's papers. Where are you from, and where bound?"

"Machias to Boston with deals, shingles, and a few barrels of salt fish."

"The port of Boston is closed, Captain. Mr. Bascomb, take a look below."

Without a word, Ike motioned toward the other document. Sparke unfolded the paper, scanned it, held it to the light. "This calls for the Captain's attention. You three stand right here and put your right hands on the binnacle. Tom, if one of them moves, use your cutlass." To the midshipman, Sparke said, "Mr. Bascomb, you are in charge until I return." He dropped down into the boat. "Give way, you two," he ordered.

Neither Chris nor Nat were used to being threatened and ordered about in this peremptory fashion, but Tom took it quite naturally and his cutlass was a formidable weapon. Captain Isaac Jones, however, resented it and showed it.

"You can just stop waving that cutlass in my face, sailor, and tell me what you are going to do."

"What I was told," replied Tom. "Just you keep your hand on that binnacle."

Midshipman Bascomb, who had just returned from a cursory look below, this time to the after cabin, put in his two pence, "and take off your hat when you are spoken to by a King's officer. Why did you try to run away when we hailed you? Didn't you see our flag?" Captain Ike very wisely kept his mouth clamped shut.

★   ★   ★

A lieutenant stepped over *Polly's* rail. He was a young man, not tall, but with an erect bearing that gave him an air of authority.

"Which one of you is Jones?"

"That one with the fancy hat," piped Bascomb.

"Mr. Bascomb, take charge of our boat." He made an impatient motion toward the starboard side. "And you can put up your cutlass, Clark."

"I am Isaac Jones, master of this vessel and well known in Boston. And you, sir?"

"Lieutenant Joshua Nunn, Captain of HMS *Halifax*. Do you know what is in this letter?"

"I do."

"How did it come into your possession?"

" The author of the letter gave it to me."

"Why?"

"Because he trusted me. Since he arrived here last year, I have been of service to him and to General Gage. I am well spoken of in Boston they tell me, and I keep my word."

"Very well, Mr. Jones, you may go on your way and I will go mine. I advise you to take good care of this letter and not to show it around." He returned the letter to Ike, moved toward the rail, then turned around abruptly. His gaze flickered over Nat and settled on Chris. "Who are you?"

"Chris MacDonald, sir."

"Where born? MacDonald sounds like a Scottish name to me."

Chris thought fast. Of course he had no idea where he was born, but he did know that citizens of the American Colonies were legally exempt from the press. To be impressed into the British Navy would be a disaster. Ruthie might well be in a family way and he was needed at home. "My father and mother lived in Newburyport, sir."

Ike didn't want to lose Chris and knew Chris was on thin ice.

"I don't believe the Admir—the author of that letter would be pleased if you pressed my mate," said Ike.

Nunn hesitated, then turned away. "Good day, Captain," he said and stepped down into the waiting boat.

Polly bore away toward Boston. Nat set the jib and trimmed the staysail to leeward. As Chris hauled in the main sheet, Ike, at the tiller, observed, "Chris, you'll have to patch that hole in the jib."

Chapter 16

Pilot

Chris was tallying the deals and boards being unloaded from *Polly* by delinquent soldiers under guard. He was comfortably seated on a pile of spruce boards in the low December sun with a stout oak tally board about an inch thick and a foot and a half long on which he marked every deal that come over the rail.

Two soldiers, a little weavy, joined the group on the wharf. One stood right in front of Chris.

"Hey, soldier, move over, will you?" No answer. No move.

"Get your big bum out of my way. I can't see the hatch."

"Who says?" grumbled the soldier.

"I say."

"Why, you little back-woods prick, don't you tell me where to stand."

"Move over." Chris gave him a shove. The soldier staggered against his companion.

"Don't push me around, you little bugger. Half nigger and half red Indian, I'll break you in two."

Chris let him have it with the tally board, a hard, solid crack on the top of the head, which split the board in two pieces and knocked the soldier against his companion.

"Help," he bellowed. "Get that damned Yankee."

Before Chris could defend himself, he was encircled from behind by strong arms, tripped up, rolled on the gravel, and kicked painfully. But it didn't last long. The officer of the guard appeared and quickly ascertained that Chris had assaulted a soldier, now bleeding copiously from the wound on his head. He marched Chris off to a shed, where he was put in irons on ankles and wrists and a bar put painfully through his elbows and across his back.

Two days later, Chris was released from irons and transferred to the jail but was still banged and bruised, exhausted, dirty, and hungry. Neither Ike nor anyone else had visited him. Despair overwhelmed him.

He worried most about Ruthie, for he knew she was in a family way and their child would be born in late February. He knew Alice and Nomi would help her, but he desperately wanted to be there and would have been, too, if he hadn't lost his temper with that drunken soldier.

Ike, who had seen the whole thing from *Polly*'s deck, waited upon Admiral Graves in a small cabin under the quarterdeck of the flagship. The admiral was not an imposing figure. Gray, rather short in stature, solidly built, he had a harried look about him, like one who knew it was going to rain but hoped it would hold off for a bit.

"Sit down, Jones, and tell me in a few words why you are here."

"Sir, my mate, Christopher MacDonald, has been arrested. I need him if I am to continue supplying you with lumber in my sloop."

"What is the charge against him?"

"No formal charges. He was outrageously insulted, resisted, and was overwhelmed and arrested."

"No charges? Hmm." The admiral thought that over. Ike

could almost see the interlocking wheels of thought turning behind the admiral's eyes.

With no charges, I can release the man without formal procedures, thought Graves. *Then Jones will owe me a favor. What do I need of Jones? Lumber. I'm getting that already. A pilot for* Halifax? *That's it.*

"Mr. Jones, I will release your mate at once on condition that you supply me with a competent pilot who knows the waters between here and Eastport." It was Ike's turn to think.

I can't give him Nat. He's too young and doesn't know the coast well enough. I can give him Eddie Bancroft off the Unity, *but he and that whole crew are flaming Whigs and would not last long in the Royal Navy. If I give him Chris, he will be happy. Nat and I can sail* Polly *home somehow and we'll find a mate somehow. And he may not need Chris for long.*

"All right, Admiral. Rather ironically, the very best pilot I have is the same Christopher MacDonald. Not only does he know every creek, harbor and eel rut between here and Eastport, but he can read a chart, set a course, and take bearings. And he is not into politics, if you know what I mean."

"Done!" said the Admiral as they shook hands on the deal. "I'll see that the orders are written today and delivered to Lieutenant Nunn. Have him go aboard as soon as possible."

Ike, bearing the Admiral's note, had Chris released, got him a good meal and a chance to clean up. Chris, with his sea bag over his shoulder, reported to Lieutenant Nunn aboard *Halifax.* He was troubled by the thought of serving in the British Navy, *but,* he thought, *anything to get home.*

Chris soon got used to *Halifax,* which was bigger than *Polly,* with heavier gear and fore and main topsails. He found Captain Nunn rather stiff, intent on his business, and running a taut ship. They had just passed Cape Elizabeth on a bright January day with an unseasonably moderate northwest breeze.

"Sail ho," called the lookout, "and this is no little fisherman."

Captain Nunn steadied his glass on her, then tucked it under his arm and mounted the main rigging. Just below the cross trees, he focused on the stranger. *A stout brig,* he said to himself. *About eighty tons, sailing toward us west-by-south. We better have a look at her.* On deck, he told the sailing master what he had seen. "We'll hold our course, Tom, about north-by-east. We'll be coming at her head on and he may not know we are Navy. Take in our flag, leave the gunports closed but be ready to clear for action."

Chris could now see that the brig was a stout little vessel, Maine built and Maine rigged, probably homeward bound from the Spanish Main. As Chris watched, she tacked, her headsails backed, and then the sails on her mainmast swung around and were trimmed on her new course, about north-northeast. *Halifax* was gaining on her fast, but she must have become suspicious and bore off to bring the wind aft, a brig's fastest point of sailing.

"Pilot, are there harbors behind Seguin, up under the shore where she could get in?"

"Yes, sir. Several," said Chris.

"Hold her to the wind, quartermaster. Tom, can't you get that foresail to draw better? It's all a-luff. Pilot, if she tacks in shore, can you take us in there?"

"Yes, sir."

An hour later *Halifax* had the brig about a mile on her lee bow.

"Hoist our colors and clear for action," called Captain Nunn.

"Open your ports," said Tom.

A cloud of smoke puffed from the stern of the brig, there was a sharp report and a crash of rending wood. Three feet of *Halifax*'s bulwark was gone.

"That's a long twelve," said Nunn. "We'll bear down on her and board. All guns hold your fire. Boarders arm yourselves." There was a rush for cutlasses and pikes.

The 12-pounder spoke again. The ball flew high. The gunner was shooting for the top of the lower masts, where all the shrouds and halyards came together.

As *Halifax* gained, the 12-pounder fired less often for the brig had to luff to bring to bear the gun mounted on her stern, and she lost much of her lead every time."

"All guns fire as you bear."

The *Halifax*'s three little 3-pounders did the best they could, but they made impressive clouds of smoke.

"Boarders," ordered Nunn.

"Quartermaster, lay me alongside her weather bow." The brig's rail now also bristled with pikes and cutlasses, but she appeared to have no more than ten or a dozen men. As *Halifax* bored in on the brig, boarders lined the rail, flourishing cutlasses and pikes and far outnumbering the brig's small crew. The brig's flag came down.

"Cease firing," called Nunn as the two vessels came together and lashings were passed.

The skipper of the brig came aboard. He was in violation of Parliament's latest law, for he was carrying rum, sugar, and molasses from St. Eustatia and fifty barrels of gunpowder from Nassau. His crew was herded forward aboard *Halifax* and confined in the fore peak under guard. The skipper was taken aft and told to put his hand on the binnacle and keep it there.

"Mr. Sparke, come below," ordered Nunn.

Installed in the cabin aft, the only place in which they
could talk confidentially, Tom asked, "What are you going to do
with these Yankees?"

"Set them ashore and let 'em go." Said Nunn regretfully.

"We lose head money that way."

"We haven't enough men to guard them and handle both
vessels, and we would have to go back to Boston to turn them
in as prisoners, and we have orders to patrol the coast from here
to Eastport.

"And we would have to feed them all the way back to
Boston. How do we get them ashore?"

"Go into Falmouth tonight and let them go ashore in
their own boat. Send the brig in to Boston as a prize. Can you
pick four men as a prize crew?"

They went back on deck to find Midshipman Bascomb
tormenting the captain.

"Thought you would get away from the Royal Navy, did
you? Your old square-built butter box of a brig just can't do it.
Yankee built is badly built."

"I made the model for that vessel myself," said the captain defensively. "I lofted her and my boys and I built her and
she is well built."

"Bah. Yankee talk. She is ours now, but the Admiralty
won't buy in a lousy American-built craft."

The midshipman rattled on, insulting American-built
boats, American builders, American seamen, and Americans in
general.

Chris, standing near, was disgusted and then not a little
angry at the ignorant young upstart in a midshipman's hat
humiliating a man who had put all he had into a venture, was
within a few miles of bringing it home, and lost it all. Of

course, Chris couldn't do anything about it, but he did say, "Give it a rest, boy."

Bascomb turned on him. "Another Yankee smart alec."

Captain Nunn came on deck. "Pilot, is there a harbour nearby where some of these people could be set ashore tonight?"

"Yes, sir, if the wind holds."

"Take us there."

Tom chose four men, sent them aboard the brig and cast off. As she braced up for Boston, her captain, hand still on the binnacle, wiped an eye and blew his nose.

"You can take your hand off the binnacle now, but why so sad, Captain?" asked Nunn. "I am going to set you and your crew ashore tonight."

"There goes all I had," said the skipper, nodding after the brig's stern, already too far away to read her name. "I'll walk home with empty pockets. Even my watch is gone."

Chris took *Halifax* into Potts Harbor and the captain and crew of the brig left in their own boats.

Chapter 17

Lieutenant Nunn's Letters

Boston
January 1, 1775

Dear Hugh,

It is long since I wrote and much has happened. I am now the captain of HM armed schooner *Halifax*. Our brother Jon is with me and also my shipmate Tom Sparke from *Active* as master's mate. *Halifax* is about sixty feet long, rigged with two square topsails. She is quite fast off the wind with her big topsails and to windward, less the topsails, she will sail within 5 1/2 points from the wind's eye.

But o' she leaks! She was built in Halifax by house carpenters, most of whom by now have died of old age. She was bought into the Navy by Admiral Hood in 1768, taken to England, fitted with topmasts too heavy for her, and armed with six 3-pounders, too small to do much execution, but heavy enough to start every bolt and treenail in her. She leaks through her seams, through her butts, and most miserably through her decks. We pump whenever we are under way.

After a trip to Halifax and back, we spent a busy summer patrolling Massachusetts Bay and were looking forward to a quiet winter in Boston harbour with nothing to do but pump when Captain Maltby put HM schooner *Glasgow* ashore off

Cohasset. We happened to be nearby, saw his rockets—it was the dead of a black night—and helped him get off. We pumped all of Boston Bay through her at least twice and grounded her out in Boston. As a reward (?), Admiral Graves thanked me, drank two glasses of hot mulled wine with me, and told me that, lacking *Glasgow,* he needed *Halifax* for the winter. He gave me orders "to patrol from Cape Elizabeth to Passamaquoddy, taking advantage of wind and weather to make unscheduled visits to various ports without my intentions being known." Of course we would need a local pilot for this, so he gave me Christopher MacDonald, mate on the sloop *Polly,* under Capt. Ichabod Jones. They had been bringing lumber from down east to build barracks for Gage's marines, wretchedly bivouacked on Boston Common. MacDonald appears to be a quiet, pleasant fellow and, I trust, an adequate pilot.

> Your h'mble etc. brother,
> Josh

Major Bagaduce
February 12, 1775

Dear Hugh,

Since the New Year we have been patrolling this arctic coast, spewing bilgewater from our scuppers constantly. We caught a Yankee brig off Falmouth with a cargo of sugar, molasses, rum and fifty barrels of gunpowder from Nassau—of course an illegal voyage. I sent her into Boston with a prize crew and set her people ashore. What else? I could neither feed them nor guard them. We laid out one cold gale in Boothbay, where a well-disposed citizen gave us a good dinner. We visited a number of coves, harbors, and islands up the bays, places that our pilot had often visited buying lumber and salt fish. The inhabitants are, in general, close-mouthed, inhospitable, and sullen. However, at the head of Penobscot Bay we anchored at this town of Major Bagaduce and were well received by loyal people. We were entertained ashore and were warm at last for a few days.

It seems a number of Americans loyal to His Majesty, who have been annoyed and even assaulted by rebels, have gathered in St. George and the villages around here to defend themselves. The rebels fit out "shaving mills," cutters, or big shallops filled with armed raiders to attack any loyalist house, wharf, or small village near the shore. If we could catch one, we'd hang them for the pirates they are. They know who we are and where we are and always slip away after they've done their dirty work. Actually, the loyal people are planning to fit out a few shaving mills themselves.

Do write me what is happening at home, in care of HMS *Preston* in Boston.

Your Obdt Svt.
Josh

Chapter 18

Sheep Island Rock
February 15, 1775

"All hands! All hands on deck to get underway. Shake a leg. Shake a leg! On deck to get underway!"

Chris groaned and stretched in his blanket, then rolled out of his hammock, stumbling over his boots as he shook the sleep out of his head.

"This crazy skipper is a wild man," complained Tommy Martley as he hit the deck out of the next hammock. Turn us out in the middle of the night to go under full sail Somewhere, arrive Nowhere, and tear off the next day to go Anywhere. Someone must have left a knife in his binnacle."

"I can take it," said Chris, "if we're bound east. That's homeward bound."

On deck, it was still black dark with the stars brilliant in a clear sky and the hills of Mt. Desert like a parade of elephants showing black in the north. Chris shivered under his watch coat and pulled his cap over his ears against the sharp northerly wind. He moved aft to the quarterdeck where Lieutenant Nunn waited impatiently.

"Pilot, we are bound east today. Can we make Machias by dark?"

Chris hedged, but hoped. "Likely, sir. This breeze will probably die out and come in sou'west, but if there is any weight in it, we should get to Machias."

Good news, good news. Homeward bound and maybe see Ruthie tonight and see how the little one is coming on. And a fair wind. And a fair wind.

Tom Sparke's sharp voice spoke up, "Get that throat halyard up taut, Webster. Put some beef on it, you two. Now the peak." Blocks squealed, ropes creaked; reef points pattered against the big mainsail. On the fo'c's'le four men were heaving in the slack on the anchor line. Chris unlashed the long tiller and tucked it under his arm. Others hoisted the foresail while Webster and Smith coiled down the main halyards.

"Up and down, sir," called the bosun.

"Stand by forestaysail halyards. Break her out." The anchor crew caught a turn on the capstan and hove around. "Hoist away on the forestaysail," called Tom.

"Anchor's aweigh, sir," called Martley from the fo'c's'le.

Two tacks took the schooner out into the Eastern Way headed east. Sparke soon had the jib and main topsail set. With the wind on her port quarter and booms out to starboard, *Halifax* swashed out across Frenchman Bay, lifting to the old roll coming in from the south. The stars, still brightly polished, moved slowly westward, the only other light the lamp in the binnacle. The watch on deck, except for the lookout forward and two men at the pump, huddled under the low break of the foredeck. Lieutenant Nunn stood rigidly on the weather side of the quarterdeck in the position of authority. Chris, with the tiller under his arm, leaned against the slight pull of *Halifax's* weather helm and watched her eat up the miles toward home.

The sky had not even begun to pale in the east when the black bulk of Schoodic Point loomed against the stars abeam. The lookout struck two bells and George came aft to relieve Chris at the tiller.

"Course east a quarter south"

"East a quarter south it is, sir."

"Where does that take us, Pilot?" asked Nunn.

"Outside 'Tit Manan, sir."

"I've heard that is a bad place."

"So it is, sir. The ledges make out a long way and there's a rock a mile outside that will be breaking today."

"Take us outside the rock, Pilot."

"Not necessary, sir. Where we can see everything today, there is plenty of room to go between the rock and the island."

"Outside the rock, Pilot."

"Very well, sir. Course east by south." Chris left the tiller and compass to George, went forward, and stood by the main rigging, choking down the comments rising bitterly in his throat. *There he goes playing admiral again. No need to go way offshore there. The tide will be fair by then and it runs hard in by the island. No use to go lallygagging around out there. What does he hire a pilot for if he knows so much? Pain in the arse.* He would have gone on had he not been so tired.

By this time the sky was beginning to show light in the east, the stars paled, and, with the coming light, the wind began to fade, although it was still a good breeze. The water swished by the lee side and Machias, though it was distant still, drew closer.

The eastern sky ahead grew brighter. The sea changed from black to grey, then for an instant to deep purple. A crumb of sun showed ahead and it was day. The lieutenant came on deck again, scanned the low shore to the north with his glass, and asked, "Is there any place along that shore, Pilot, where one of those Yankee Doodles could hide?"

"Not much, sir. There is a little settlement at Prospect

Harbor, but you can see right into that now and two long bays up into the land, but it would take a long time to beat up in there and then this wind will shift and it would take a long time to beat out again." The Lieutenant scanned along the shore again and clapped his glass to, looked aloft and back at the wake, and called, "Mr. Sparke, foretopsail."

The low white island of Petit Manan slid by to port, outlined by a dark line of weed and a white line of breakers, breakers that stretched a long finger southward.

"Pilot, are we clear of that rock outside? I don't see it."

"Yes, sir. You can see it break once in a while about one point forward of the port beam."

"Very well."

Six bells struck. "Relieve the helm and lookout!"

"Course east by north," Chris told the new man at the tiller.

"East by north it is, sir." They steered for an empty horizon, the cliffs of Crumple Island twelve miles away invisible in the sun's glare.

Gradually the breeze faded, the water just whispered by. The schooner took a roll to windward. The main sheet dropped slack and snapped taut again as she rolled back. Smoke from the galley ducked under the fore boom and spread lazily over the silky sea to southward. A slow hour passed.

At eight bells, "Cooks to the galley" was called. There followed the usual rush and clatter of mess gear. Chris went below and joined the bosun, gunner, carpenter, and surgeon eating oatmeal, and hard bread, and drinking coffee under the break of the quarterdeck.

"Take good care of us, Chris," said the carpenter. "This old barky won't stand much of a rap on a rock. They caulked some butts a while back, but the oakum went right through into the bilge."

"He'll take care of us," replied the surgeon. "He wants to get home tonight."

"Where's home? It makes no odds to me. All these little mud holes look the same."

"Not to me," said Chris. But he did not elaborate and conversation turned to hard times under a Lieutenant Rogers of recent memory.

On deck again, Chris found the sea stark calm, not a breath stirring, and *Halifax* rolling broadside to the swell, slamming her sheet blocks on the deck, slatting the limp sails, and swilling the water gushing from the pump from scupper to scupper. He went aft to look at the compass.

"No steerage way, sir."

Nunn was looking off to port with his glass again. "What's that bay, Pilot?"

"We call it Narraguagus Bay. It goes way up into the land behind those high islands."

"Any towns or harbors?"

"There's several good harbors, sir, but no towns to amount to much until you come to Milbridge, where there's several sawmills." Nunn turned to peering through his glass again and Chris was relieved that he had asked nothing about Mooseabec Reach and the inside passage. Chris turned his back and searched the southern horizon. No sign of a breeze, but he noticed that the Mt. Desert hills had lost their sharp outlines and now loomed a dusty blue. *Won't be long now,* he said to himself.

The sun, now well up in the southern sky, had taken the bite out of the air. It felt almost like spring. Chris leaned back against the main rigging. He was tired. It had been a long day yesterday. In his zeal to capture smugglers, the Lieutenant had brought them from Castine through Eggemoggin Reach, down into Burntcoat Harbor. Then they'd had to beat the long way back up to Mount Desert and Cranberry Harbor. Of course they had seen no smugglers, for the word was out that they were on the coast. As Chris's mind went back through yesterday's run, his head dropped, his eyelids drooped. Before he quite dropped off, he was jolted awake by:

"Pilot, look alive there. When is this southerly wind coming in?"

"Should be any time now, sir. It's seldom calm for long in February."

Sweet Jesus; how in hell should I know when the wind is going to blow? The wind bloweth where it listeth, and I hope it listeth pretty soon. He stood up and again studied the southern horizon. On the pale sea there at last appeared a hard dark line. As Chris watched, it crept closer, grew broader. He smelled a faint cold breath of sea air. The booms creaked across to the port side. The jibs backed and slowly swung *Halifax* to port.

"Trim jibs to port. Topsail braces," called Tom Sparke. By the time the watch on deck had trimmed sails, the faint air had become a light breeze. *Halifax* came to life again, swung on to her east-by-north course, and again the sea whispered, then swished, along her lee side. Petit Manan dropped out of sight astern. Crumple Island and Great Wass Island rose on the port bow. The new breeze built in quickly.

"What's that breaking to leeward, Pilot?

"Sea Horse Rock, sir, and Seal Ledges."

"Do they extend this way?"

'No, sir."

"What about that island ahead?"

"Crumple Island and Great Wass, sir. Steep as the side of a barn and the flood tide runs hard close in shore. Going our way, sir."

"Very well, Pilot."

Going our way. Going our way and home today.

Sea Horse Rock came abeam and passed astern. The white cliffs of Crumple Island, the deep cut of Main Channel Way, and the high land of Head Harbor Island slid by. The southwest breeze, more westsouthwest really, was building in fast and building up a sea with it. *Halifax* was now rushing eastward as fast as she would ever go, lifting her stern to every wave and spreading a wide fan of white water ahead of her blunt bow. The pumps were going again as the leaks increased with the strain. Both Lieutenant Nunn and Tom Sparke were on deck now, watching with some concern topmasts and topsail yards bending, sheets bar taut, masts and rigging creaking.

"She won't stand a great deal of this, Mr. Sparke. Take in the main topsail."

"Aye, aye, sir."

In the commotion of getting in the topsail, Chris studied the shore where the rocks changed from white to black. He made out the bare mast of a sloop in the cove behind the first big black rock. *Probably Ike Jones's sloop.* But he said nothing about it. This was no time to stop and examine a captain's papers.

As Black Head drew abeam—the little schooner was flying now—Chris asked, "Lieutenant, we must haul up to the north now. Do we gybe or tack?"

"Mr. Sparke, tack ship. It would be asking too much of her to gybe in this wind and sea."

"All hands to tack ship." It took the full crew with men on jib sheets, foretopsail sheets and braces, fore and main sheets.

As the helmsman eased her around to starboard and she took the wind abeam, she filled her lee deck and threw several hogsheads of frigid water over her bow. The crew on the main sheet—four men and the cook—trimmed in sharply, she came to the wind, sails, booms, and blocks slamming wildly, fell off to starboard, gathered way, and swung off on her new course, mainsail to starboard, foresail to port, winged out for home.

In the smoother water under Head Harbor Island she ran much more easily. Ahead lay the islands of Machias Bay. Chris had considered going outside around the Brothers and the round domes of the Scabby Islands, but chose the shorter and more sheltered course inside Pulpit Rock, around Sheep Island and inside Foster's Island, where Ben Foster ran his sheep in the summer.

"Pilot, can you find someone in Machias to take us to Passamaquoddy when we get in?" asked Nunn. Chris thought briefly that it would be fun to mention one of the O'Brien boys. They would tell that stiff-necked lieutenant that King George did not have enough money to buy one of them. It would be an interesting confrontation, but he reconsidered.

"Yes, sir. You could probably get one of the Libby boys. They go down that way quite often—or maybe Ben Foster."

Although the sea was less, that big old roll from the south hurried *Halifax* on her way and Chris could feel Ruthie pulling on the string. He had waited so long, seen so many delays, and at last he was closing in on it. He hoped he was in time.

"Pilot, I see a breaker quite close to port. Keep her off."

"Sir, I know that ledge well. Fished all around it. It doesn't make out at all. And off to starboard is another. We call it the Jumper. Hasn't moved a bit since I was a boy. We'll run around

Pulpit Rock, by Sheep Island, and run up the bay. We should be anchoring in a little over half an hour."

"Mr. Sparke, take in the fore topsail and range the anchor line on deck."

As Pulpit Rock sped by to starboard, Chris called out from the tiller, "Stand by to tack again, sir." Again they tacked ship, this time under easier circumstances, and ran along the shore of Sheep Island under what was still a strong breeze.

Sheep Island Rock should be breaking, but it's high water and a moon tide too. I guess its somewhere over there to port.

"Pilot, are we far enough off that island? Things look pretty tight in here."

0' my soul. Playing admiral again! To the devil with him. We must be outside the rock. I'm tired and I'm going home.

"It's all right, sir." *Halifax* lifted her stern on a sea, it broke under her and dropped her with a hard jolt. The tiller swung across and hit Chris a hard blow under the ribs. She bounced ahead, struck again forward and swung around to starboard, sails and booms thrashing. Chris lay in the scuppers where the tiller had thrown him, his wind knocked out, unable to talk. *My God! The Rock!*

Chapter 19
More of Nunn's Letters

Off Black Head, Head Harbour Island
February 15, 1775

Dear Hugh,

That northwester built up to half a gale. We beat up toward the Mt. Desert hills, a long board and a short one, under close-reefed mainsail, foresail, and forestaysail. It was cold, but the sun is getting higher, and in the lee of the islands the sea was smooth and we made good progress. We anchored before dark in Southwest Harbour. The next morning we inspected every vessel there. The word is out now that we are on the coast, so of course we found nothing. Gunpowder? They professed to know nothing about gunpowder. Such innocent people I have never seen!

Yesterday we came across to Cranberry Harbour, whence we could leave at night without anyone knowing where we were headed. By 3 a.m. the northwester had eased up some, so we left on the last of the ebb and headed east. I plan to get to Machias tonight, leave our pilot, who professes to be ignorant of the coast east of that place, pick up another pilot, and go on to Passamaquoddy. I will show the flag there and then work back westward, visiting places that we have missed bound east.

About 9 o'clock this morning, the wind died and then came in again from the WSW very fresh. We are now running 7 knots before an old roll and a growing chop, and pumping vigorously. This is a wicked coast with a heavy surf on high black cliffs.

Six bells.

More later.

Boston, February 25

We lost *Halifax*! We struck a rock up Machias Bay. It was all the fault of that damned pilot. I don't know where he is now, but I hope that it is a lot hotter there than he would like it. I just got back here and will write you a full account later. No one hurt and Jon is all right.

Hastily, y'r h'mble etc. brother,

Joshua

Boston, March 1

Dear Hugh,

Here is the tale of a shipwreck in brief. We were running up Machias Bay before a half a gale from WSW. We had just tacked and were running along the shore of Sheep Island when a sea broke under us and let us down with a smash on a rock. She bounced ahead, swung around broadside to the wind, dropped into a cleft in the rock, and there she is now, what is left of her. The pilot, who was steering at the time, was on his hands and knees in the starboard scuppers, quite delirious. We tried to get her off, all quite in vain. She was all awash below and firmly lodged. Fortunately, no one was hurt.

I got the boats out and we carried ashore everything we could, rigged a shelter of sorts with sails and spars, and built several fires of driftwood. When the tide went, we found she was hopelessly stove and had begun to break up. At about 8 o'clock, as the tide came, she fell over on her beam ends and the seas washed right over her mastheads.

We spent a rather miserable night. It rained and snowed and blew hard. Our "tents" were not waterproof and slatted about in the wind so no one slept much, but by morning it moderated some. The vessel had broken up and nothing showed except her masts floating to leeward of the rock.

I sent Tom with our one remaining boat—the other was stove during the night—to get help, and of course I had to send the pilot with him. When he recovered the power of speech, he said he knew of the rock, that it was usually visible or at least it broke, but that it was dead high water on a moon tide and he had been unable to see it. He guessed we were outside it. He said he was sorry! I told Tom not to lose sight of him and sent them off for help.

Meanwhile we salvaged what we could of what was driven ashore from the wreck. The next day Tom came back in a little schooner belonging to one Sam Beale, but without the pilot. Tom said that they had arrived at Bucks Harbor after a long, cold, wretched passage. While Tom was away hunting up Capt. Beale, the pilot slipped away. In my opinion, he was very well advised to do so.

We loaded what we could aboard the schooner and Beale

took us to Machias, where I was able to charter a big sloop to bring us back to Boston, and here we are. There will, of course, be a court martial. I will write you about it if I can. What a way to end my first command!

Boston
March 10, 1775

Dear Hugh,

The court martial is over. I am acquitted and everyone else declared blameless. The pilot was judged solely responsible. I am given command of the cutter *Folkstone* and to be sent home with dispatches, so will see you soon and give you all the details.

It was rather a strange proceeding. The day before, when I was a "prisoner" aboard *Somerset,* the admiral's secretary came to acquaint me with the proper procedure and emphasized that I was to answer only such questions as were asked and to volunteer nothing. Apparently other witnesses were given the same advice.

The court elicited the story of the wreck, determined that the pilot was alone responsible, and adjourned. No one asked the pilot's name, whence he came, or where he went. Admiral Graves knows who he was, for the Admiral appointed him and it would add nothing to his already shaky record if the pilot came to trial. Also, the pilot had been mate of a sloop carrying lumber under license from the admiral to build barracks for Gage's marines and the admiral may have been reluctant to disturb that connection.

Jon is well and was not called at the court martial. He will be with me in *Folkstone*. Tom Sparke has a pleasant berth aboard *Preston* as an aide to the admiral, although he is still rated Masters Mate.

I look forward to seeing you in blossom time.

Your hmble etc. brother,
Josh

Chapter 20

Surprise!

Chris lay in the starboard scuppers, gasping for breath, for the tiller had completely knocked the wind out of him. Captain Nunn had pitched forward over the low break of the quarterdeck and the working party forward had all been thrown flat. The next sea lifted *Halifax*'s stern and drove her ahead. She swung to starboard into a cleft in the rock in a flurry of suds and lay there, hard aground with fore and mainsails thundering.

"Anybody hurt?" called the captain as soon as he got to his feet.

"No, sir," answered Sparke from forward. And no spars carried away.

"Get the fore and main sails off her, ordered Nunn, and back jib and staysail to starboard. Carpenter, is there water in the well?

"She's stove in forward, sir. Rotten as a punkin. She'll never float again."

Then turning to Chris, who was still gasping for breath, "Pilot, what island is this?"

Chris crept to his knees, raised his head to look over the port rail, and gasped incoherently.

"Come, pilot, What is the name of this island?

"Sh— Sh— Shep—"

"How far to Machias?"

"About ten miles, sir," gurgled Chris.

"Is there a place to land on the island?"

"Y—Yes, sir. There's a good little cove on the west end and an open bight on the east end."

"How did you come to hit the rock? Did you know it was there?"

"Fished all around it. Usually breaks. Top of the moon tide. Thought we were clear of it. I'm awful sorry, sir. Real sorry."

"You're sorry! Well, you'll be sorrier. Clarke," he hailed a seaman. "Don't let this fellow out of your sight. Not out of your sight! Understand, Clarke?"

Halifax lay on her port side, the seas washing up into her port scuppers. Fore and main halyards had been slacked and the gaffs lay on the booms, the booms in the water, and the slack sails washing around them. The passing seas had ceased to lift her and drop her on the ledge. She was a sorry sight, disheveled and mortally wounded.

As the tide ebbed, the crew ferried provisions ashore, water and gear. A party ashore on the east end set up fore and mainsails as shelters and rigged a fireplace for the cook. Chris was kept busy aboard under Clarke's eye.

Just before dark, Captain Nunn and Sparke got out on the rock and walked around the wreck. *Halifax* had struck first about amidships, had broken her back, swung round as she charged forward, torn off her rudder, dropped into the cleft in the rock, and fell over on her port side, where she now lay.

It was a miserable night ashore. The wind shifted into the southeast and brought wet snow and rain. It blew in under the makeshift tent, but did little to drive out the smoke from the fire. After a rough supper of boiled salt beef and hard tack, all hands turned in, covering themselves with the smaller sails against the cold wind and leaky tent. Clarke was relieved of Chris and Chris ordered to bed down between Nunn and Sparke and not to move.

At first light, after a long night, Nunn and Sparke arose, ordered Chris to keep close to them, and walked up the gentle rise to where they could see the wreck. The rock showed black and angry, with nothing of *Halifax* but her stern post jammed still erect in the rock and her masts still tethered by their rigging, afloat to leeward. The shore was littered with such wreckage as the southeaster had driven in during the night. They contemplated it glumly. Chris wanted to say again he was sorry, but it seemed so inadequate. They turned and went back to the tent.

"Tom, I'll have to send you in the long boat for help."

"Long boat's stove, sir. They didn't haul her up high enough last night, but the gig's all right."

You'll have to take that, then, and four men to row, and go up the bay to Machias."

"Where's Machias? I'll need the pilot."

"Pilot, how do we get from here to Machias?"

"You go about north-northeast through the ledges around Foster's Island and across the bar into Larrabees Cove—"

"Hold it, Pilot. You'll have to take him, Tom, but don't let him slip away. He owes us our schooner."

"We would do well to start soon, sir, to get the full run of the flood tide up the bay," said Chris.

It was a miserable trip. The wind had moderated, but left a slop of a sea confused by the islands, ledges and half-tide rocks, and by the flood tide. Frequently two waves would come together, peak up, and fall in over the gig's low side, wetting an oarsman with very cold water. Tom was kept busy bailing while Chris steered. Chris had rowed up through these waters many times and knew every rock, ledge, and islet, but to Tom and the others, one half-tide rock looked much like another and they were sure Chris was lost. The men at the oars found it hard work, although Chris and Tom spelled them as much as they could. But it was small relief, for those not rowing had to bail to keep the gig afloat. At last they crossed the bar at Larrabee's Cove and found smoother water and a little easier going, but all six were tired, thirsty, hungry, and very cold and wet. When at last, against the first of the ebb tide, they fought their way into Bucks Harbor, they were six exhausted men.

Chris guided them to a stony beach in front of Howard Beal's house. They had not strength enough to pull the gig up, but anchored her with a beach rock. They staggered up the shore and Chris knocked. Howard was not home, but Betty took them in and built up the fire. They welcomed the heat. They also welcomed the rum and hot water that warmed them from the inside and slowly they began to thaw out. Tom Sparke was the first to recover.

"We are very grateful to you, ma'am, for your hospitality. We were nearly frozen as it was and you have saved us. Our schooner was wrecked yesterday on Sheep Island. Is there anyone in town who could pick up our shipmates?"

"Oh, yes. My husband Howard could get them in his schooner. He is up to the Port right now, but I am sure he would help you. Just follow the path around the head of the harbor when you are ready. It's about three miles." Tom took another drink of the hot water and rum, picked up a piece of bread that Betty offered, and struck out. Betty saw him to the door, closely followed by Chris. As she closed the door behind Tom, she turned to Chris.

"You're Chris MacDonald, aren't you? What are you doing with these Navy fellows?"

"I'm the pilot that wrecked their schooner."

"You are? Well done!"

"I didn't do it a-purpose—"

"That don't make no nevermind. Wait here for ten minutes and let him get out of sight and then slip out. I'll get you a mug of soup and a hunk of bread. Those fellas," she gestured over her shoulder, "won't go anywhere for a while." The soup and bread were strengthening, and Chris slipped out, homeward bound.

The next afternoon, Chris was striding along the path from the Port to Machias. Knowing that Sparke was inquiring for Howard Beal at the Port, he had circled around the Port and harbor, struck the path above the town, and was now stretching it out for home. *What was Ruthie's state? Had the baby come yet? Was everything all right?*

He heard the clumping of a horse's hooves behind him and ducked behind a bush, lest Sparke had sent a party out looking for him. As the horse came closer, however, he saw that the rider was Jerry O'Brien, eldest of Morris O'Brien's boys and an eager Son of Liberty. Chris stepped out and hailed him.

"Jerry, any news of Ruthie and my family?"

"I don't know. I been down at the Port. I hear that damned British schooner that's been nosing around the coast to the west'ard got wrecked on Sheep Island."

"I know."

"How do you know?"

"I was there. It was all my fault. High water on a moon tide and the rock wasn't breaking. I was in a hurry to get home and that captain kept bugging me with questions and I cut it too close."

"Great work, Chris. That schooner's been a nuisance all up the coast. Took George Eldridge's *Ann* off Casco Bay with powder, shot, and muskets aboard. You ought to get a medal, Chris, but at least I can give you a ride. Old Sparky can carry two."

"But I didn't do it a-purpose."

"Who cares? Get aboard."

Jerry let Chris off in front of his house and rode off to spread the good news, which traveled fast. Chris hurried up the hill. As he approached the door, he heard what he took for a nest of young crows cawing. He opened the door and stopped short. Alice and Ruthie faced him, grinning like cats. Ruthie threw herself on him, hugging him tight without a word. He could hardly get his breath.

"What happened? Was it good? Are you all right?"

"She's better than all right," chortled Alice, "she's magnif-icent, and you are the father of two brand-new twin boys, Albert and John. Come see." Alice and Ruthie led Chris to a jury-rigged crib from which each picked up a tiny baby.

"Twins," said Ruthie. "This is John with the big ears and this is Albert. Here" she said, "You hold John. Hold his head up. He isn't very strong yet." Chris held John's tiny head in his broad hand and the rest of his son along his forearm. John looked Chris curiously right in the eye and Chris was sudden-ly enormously proud of John, Albert, and Ruthie. He was a family man! Now Albert was cawing for attention and Chris gave him his full share.

Ian came in from the shop, glanced over at the twins as if to be sure they were still there. "Welcome home, Chris. You must have had some trip! We heard from Ike that you had been

made pilot of *Halifax*. Now there's a squad of your . . . ah . . .
friends outside come to call on you." There was confused
shouting outside and a hearty knock on the door. Ian opened
it and stood squarely in front of it, suspicious of the cause of the
visit. Jerry O'Brien confronted him with a grin.

"The Sons of Liberty have come to welcome Chris
home. We have a seat saved for him at the Wildcat Inn."

"Hurrah for Chris—the only one who has done anything to slow up the British."

"Three cheers. All together now." Little Fox led them,
with Big Dan adding real volume. Chris stepped by his father.

"I didn't mean to do it. It was all a mistake," he protest-
ed. But Jerry, his brother John, Big Dan, and Red Larrabee
hoisted Chris to their shoulders and bore him off to the inn.
The room soon filled.

'Tell us, Chris, how did you do it so neatly?"

"No people killed."

"No one even hurt."

"How did you hit that rock right on when it wasn't
breaking?"

"Did you know it was there?"

"What did the captain say?"

"How bad was she stove up? Can we float her?"

Chris didn't have a chance to answer until Jerry bellowed,
"Pipe down! Pipe down! Let Chris tell his story."

"We left Cranberry Island about three yesterday morning," began Chris.

"Get on with it!"

"Off Black Head it breezed up real fresh west-southwest
and the tide was still flooding. We ran up the bay, tacked around
Pulpit Rock. I was coming up the inside passage. Top of a

moon tide and I cut it too close and that's all there is to it."

"A likely tale!"

"Tell it to the soldiers," Big Dan called, climbing on a table. "Glenn, rum all 'round and a health to Chris, our man of action!" There was a rush to the bar, but Ben Foster sought out Chris, now deserted.

"Chris, do you mean it? Was it really a mistake?"

"Yes it was. A bad mistake. I was hired to pilot that vessel safely to Machias and I failed, and if the British don't catch up with me and hang me . . . "

"Maybe you haven't been paying attention to what has been going on in Boston."

"No, I haven't. All I want to do is go to sea . . ." Chris brought himself up short. *What about John and Albert and Ruthie?* "But I have a family now. I can't get them into all this arguing and fighting. I have to keep out of it."

"Let's talk about it later. Some of us have been getting letters from the Committee in Boston—Jerry and me and your father and some of the others. This is much more than a political difference and a riot."

"Viva Chris MacDonald!" somebody shouted.

"Hurray for the Sons of Liber*tay*."

"Drink deep. No heel taps here."

In the ensuing confusion, Chris went home. He found Ian and Alice waiting up. "You needn't tell me, Chris. I was there," said Ian. "We have lots to talk about."

"Sleep on it first, boy," said Alice.

Chapter 21

The Loon

Chris, Jackie, and Ian were working in the spar shop, a long, narrow ell, longer than the front of the house. A vise bench lay along one side, with a wide view of the river through two good glass windows. The other side had wooden shutters that could be opened in summer. A door at one end opened into the house and at the other end a door opened out, through which logs could be carried in and spars carried out. This morning, Ian was planing the corners off a twenty-foot pine boom. Chris was trimming up a knotty spruce stick with a draw knife and Jackie was fashioning oak chocks to hold the rigging on Ian's boom. The floor was cluttered with fragrant chips and shavings of spruce and pine. Work was going forward apace.

"Well, Chris, what happens now?" asked Ian between long strokes of his plane.

"I suppose they will come after me and hang me if I can't hide," said Chris. "I failed in my duty and I am a deserter. They hang deserters."

"They'll never get you," said Jackie. "They'd have to send three or four men for you and we'd see them coming or hear them in the woods. And the woods have lots of places to hide."

"I don't much like the woods," said Chris, "but that may be what I'll have to do. Will they bother Ruthie and the boys do you think?"

"I don't think so!" said Ian emphatically. "The Sons of Liberty, if I have to lead them myself, will escort the British squad to their boat and shove them off. Besides, the British have plenty to do in Boston. The new customs commissioners getting paid by Parliament are appointing new collectors whose palms are not so easily crossed and people resent having cargoes seized. One officer who tried it got tarred and feathered just last year and they had to bring two regiments into Boston to keep the Sons of Liberty under control. Nothing short of a small British army could invade Machias."

"I can't go back with Ike because I can't show up in Boston and I can't go to Falmouth and sign on for a West Indies voyage and leave Ruthie and the boys here alone."

The plane curled off long shavings and Chris hacked away at the spruce knots.

"Pa, can I stay and work with you?"

"You surely can, but the spar business is slack and getting slacker. Where the new government in Massachusetts and also that Congress in Philadelphia have ordered a non-importation agreement against England and England has said we can't trade with any other country, there isn't much need for new ships, and I don't want to build spars for British ships."

"They pay, don't they."

"I don't want to see my good Maine spars in a British frigate seizing our ships and attacking our towns."

"Has it come to that?"

"You were in *Halifax* when she took *Ann* and left Eldridge with . . . nothing."

"And stole his watch, too! That stringy Midshipman Bascomb was showing it around proudly. Said no rebel deserved to have a watch like that."

"Just where do you stand in this conflict anyway, Chris?" You talked like a Tory last night."

"I'm no Tory. I'm not anything. I'm not even an American. I'm not a Son of Liberty either, who throws tea overboard, sacks the governor's house, attacks customs officers, and goes about looting and beating people in the name of liberty. I'll do my work, draw my pay, and do nothing to offend anyone. I will not expose Ruthie and the boys to rioting and violence on either side, and if that isn't good enough for you, it isn't good enough." In his passion, Chris threw down his draw knife and brought his fist down hard on the bench.

"Easy boy, easy," said Ian. "There is more to this situation than you know. Let's take the rest of the morning off and go over to the Inn and talk with some level-headed people who know what's going on to the west'ard."

Jackie picked up the draw knife. "You've spoiled the edge on her," he said. "Take the stone and edge her up a bit." Chris took the knife, saw the edge was turned, and sat on a sawhorse to hone it up. When he finished, he shaved the hair on his arm, set the tool down carefully on the bench, and went into the house.

Ruthie had just finished nursing John and was holding him over her shoulder. "Pick up Albert, Chris, and do something useful. He'll want to burp again." As Chris picked him up, Albert did burp and smiled a toothless smile, then he seized Chris's little finger and tried to put it in his mouth.

"What are we going to do for a house?" asked Ruthie. "We can't all live here."

"We'll have to find a place, or build one. We have some money saved up and good credit at the store."

After dinner, leaving Jackie to fasten the chocks on the

new boom, Chris and Ian rowed across the river in Chris's boat *Alice*, which Ian had maintained to come and go while Chris was at sea. Halfway across, Chris rested on his oars to watch a loon, striking in his black and white uniform. The loon paid no attention to *Alice*; he had important business of his own. He ducked his head under, came up, then dove under again and vanished, leaving only a glimpse of disappearing tail feathers and a circular ripple. Chris let *Alice* drift, intently watching the smooth surface of the river for the loon to come up. Then he rowed gently on, still watching. Suddenly the loon re-appeared. Neither man saw him come up. He just materialized thirty yards downstream with a smelt crossways in his bill, gave a flip to his neck and swallowed the smelt head first. Chris rowed on and they tied *Alice* to the top of the ladder on the wharf. As they walked up the bank, the loon laughed his mysterious quavering laugh. Both paused, turned to look across the still water to the far bank, to their house with the long ell of the spar shop.

How quickly feelings strike! Both men, neither born in America, were swept by the conviction that this was their home, in their country; their own country where their children and grandchildren would live and grow up.

At the inn, they went into the east room, an addition built to provide a smaller and more private meeting place than the main room. There was a glass window looking toward the river, a bench, a rectangular table, and several neatly built chairs. The room had a hint of elegance about it, yet still smelled of the saw. At the table sat Ben Foster and Ephraim Chase discussing the siege of Louisbourg.

" . . . and we picked up the French cannonballs while they were still rolling and fired them right back where they came from."

Jerry O'Brien and Ed Weston were standing by the door into the kitchen. " . . . they could send a couple of launches up the river and burn the town before our boys could come out of the woods to defend us," said Si.

"Don't you believe it," said Jerry. "We'll see— Hello, Ian. I hoped you'd come over and bring Christopher. He is the only man of us thus far who has done anything to discommode our enemies. Sit down. I am just back from a jaunt to Falmouth, Pownalborough, Brunswick, Westport, Wiscasset, and Boothbay. The towns have been very slow to sign The Solemn League and Covenant."

"What's that?" asked Chris.

"You *are* out of it," said Ephraim. "Last summer the Provincial Congress—"

"What's that?" asked Chris.

"Last spring, General Gage, the new Governor of Massachusetts, dissolved the Great and General Court, but they didn't dissolve," Jerry responded. "They met in Salem and then in Concord and drew up a covenant refusing to trade with Britain. Many towns and people signed it, but those who didn't, Sam Thompson and his boys roughed them up. They even got that old skinflint Richard King of our old town of Scarborough. They got him up on a tar barrel, forced him to make a speech for the covenant, and sacked his house. They drove the Anglican minister out of Pownalborough, and one man—they made him dig his grave and stand in it and aimed a pistol at him, but he still refused, so they had to let him go."

"What does the Reverend Lyons have to say about all this?" asked Ed.

"I asked him," said Ephraim. "He said, 'Let your yea be yea and your nay be nay.' I said 'What does that mean? Are you with us or against us?' He said. 'Whatsoever the Lord puts into your hand to do, do it with your might. That sounds to me like he's for us."

"What does this Provincial Congress want?" pursued Chris.

"They want to govern Massachusetts and show Britain that we won't pay taxes to them," answered Jerry.

"Well, not exactly," said Ben. "They are saying we want to mind our own business, that we will not be governed by a British general, British soldiers, and by sheriffs and customs agents and officers paid from London whose cases against Americans will be tried in British courts."

"What has all that to do with us?" responded Chris. "There are no sheriffs and customs collectors here or even mast agents. Why do we have to mix into Boston or Pownalborough business? I don't really care who is the governor in Boston."

"You should," said Ian. We ship our wood to Boston, Newburyport, and Falmouth and from there comes almost everything we eat and wear, and all at a price controlled by the British." Chris was beginning to feel that he was being pushed around by people he respected, and he resented it.

"What are you going to do about it?" he challenged. "We probably have a few Tories in town. Shall we beat them up and sack Steve Jones's store?"

"No," said Jerry. "Steve has been good to all of us, but we can refuse to buy English tea and English lead from him. And one more thing, we can set up a liberty pole like lots of other towns to show we will not stand for tyranny. We stand for liberty."

"Let's wait a bit," said Ed. "No one but us is going to see it this winter and there's four feet of frost in the ground. Let's wait at least until the frost is out."

Welcoming the resolution to do nothing right away, the meeting adjourned to the bar.

Chapter 22

The Machias Gun Club

It was a cool, cloudy day in early March. The trees along the river bank were still bare. The muddy, salty smell of the flats wafted up the river on a gentle southerly breeze. Ruthie and Chris sat on the doorstep in front of the house. Albert and John had just been fed and for the time being were both quietly asleep. Chris had something on his mind, but, characteristically, was reluctant to plunge into it. But it had to be done.

"Ruthie, we've got to move."

"I know," said Ruthie, "the boys are growing faster than the house. So what are we going to do?"

"We've got no money to buy a house and land."

"So we build a house," said Ruthie. "Where and how and with what money?"

"I'll ask around."

The next day, in the manner of March days, was cold and raw with a northeast wind and a fine rain with occasional flakes of snow in it. Big Dan, Foxy (not Little Foxy any more), Sam, Jerry O'Brien, and Bill Campbell had somehow found business in the store not far from the stove.

"Hard old day to work in the woods," said Bill Campbell, now a burly young man with a sandy beard. "I suppose we could go out and cut a few trees, though," he added unenthusiastically.

"Not much sense to it," said big Dan. "Couldn't move a sledge now the snow is just slush and the oxen would slip in the mud."

"Just stay where you are, boys," put in Steve Jones, the storekeeper. "Uncle Ike's got enough logs to last him a long time." They all paused to listen to the syncopated stamp of the mills at the falls.

"Wonder if there's anything worth bringing home from the wreck of the *Halifax* down to Sheep Island," said Foxy.

"Well," said Jerry decisively as if he had been thinking it over for some time, "There's the guns. Four 3-pounder guns. Anyone know where they are? They ought to be worth a good deal."

"Chris knows as well as anyone. He was there."

The door latch rattled. "Speak of the devil …" said someone, and Chris stepped in.

"Come in and set a while," said Steve. "No one's doing anything today. How's the twins?"

"John and Albert? They're doing fine, but I can't stay. I've come to see Ike about a job in his mill. I got to have a house."

"Tell you what," said Jerry, seeing just the chance he needed, "How about the four 3-pounders on the wreck? Do you know where they are, Chris?"

"I could guess. They can't have moved far. If the rough seas in the past week haven't rolled the wreck off into the deep water, we should be able to find them."

"Would you go down with us, Chris, and drag a grapple around and see if we could find them?"

"I dunno. I got things to do."

"We could go shares, divide what we get equally. It might be worth your while. Better than working in the mill."

"How much does one of those things weigh?" asked Dan.

"A whole lot. Maybe four of us could carry one. It would be a heavy load for a bateau, but Chris's boat could carry one," said Jerry.

"You haven't even found one yet, say nothing of getting it up and hauling it here. It's a waste of time. Let King George get his own guns," said Sam truculently.

"What would you do with a 3-pounder gun if you got it?" asked Steve. " 'Good morning, Admiral Graves. Would you like to buy a cannon today?' And what would he say? 'That's the King's cannon. Bring it here to Boston right away, you damned rebel.' "

"I'm for trying it anyway," said Jerry enthusiastically. We could use the guns ourselves. Four 3-pounders mounted at the Rim could knock out any boat small enough to sail up our river. We could do it somehow. We know the guns are there. Let's go find 'em. You'll help us, won't you, Chris?" Chris nodded slowly and Jerry continued, "Anyone else want to join the Machias Gun Club?"

Foxy spoke right up. "Dan, you could carry one of those guns by yourself."

"Sure," said Dan, "with you riding on it if you didn't drag your feet."

And thus was the Machias Gun Club formed.

On the first calm, warm day, Chris, Jerry, Foxy, and Dan rowed down to the rock in *Alice* and a bateau. It was close to low water when they arrived and they found the rock was bigger than they had thought. It extended under water some distance to the north toward the island, the shore of which was littered with fragments of *Halifax*. Her two masts lay at the high water mark, still bound together by rigging. Her bowsprit lay nearby and a big piece of her stern lay awash, the sternpost still attached. But no guns.

They searched the edge of the ledge on the north side, peering down into the cold, clear water.

"Not much here," said Dan. "I don't see any guns."

"There's a big piece of the deck," said Foxy. "Must be something holding it down or it would have floated ashore. Paddle a bit to the east'd, Jerry." After a careful look through the ripply water, he said, "take me back to the west'd." The water was smoother in the lee of the ledge. Foxy pushed the floating suds away. "I think that's one of 'em. Yup, it is." Jerry leaned over the side of the bateau to see. The tiddly bateau lurched and took a big gulp of water over the side. The second time Jerry was more careful and saw the gun, too.

Chris had made a grapple of four big halibut hooks lashed together with a cod sinker to carry it down. He lowered it over the stern of *Alice*, with Dan at the oars and Jerry and Foxy watching from the bateau. The water was not only ripply, but as the tide came, a surge washed around the rock from both sides.

"Slack away, Chris. Now a little toward the rock," coached Jerry. Dan swung the stern a bit, but a sea coming around the end of the rock set *Alice* in toward the shore. "Haul it up a little, Chris. A little more to the east'd, Dan. That's good. Slack away, Chris. Now, row in toward the island, Dan, easy like. Now take a strain on it, Chris."

"I got it. I got it. I can feel the sinker coming over the gun. Now the hooks. Oh, damn! I lost it!"

The hooks could not catch on the round iron gun. They tried again and yet again. At last Chris took a strain and the grapple held.

It was getting late in the afternoon and the water was rougher. Jerry shaded his eyes and said, "What you've got,

Chris, is a piece of the deck. We can't lift that."

"Better buoy the line and leave it for today," said Chris. He tied a stick to the line and, boosted by the tide, they rowed up the river.

Chris and Ruthie talked it over with Ian and Alice. "We ought to move," said Ruthie.

"You are welcome to stay on here as long as you want," said Alice, looking around the room crowded with a double crib, two beds, a table, four chairs, orderly piles of clothes and cooking gear and drying diapers. "But it is getting pretty snug."

"You do need a place of your own," said Ian. "It's time you flew the nest."

"Do you think if we can get those guns up, it will be enough to get me started?" asked Chris.

"Might be," said Ian. "It's a gamble. How hard is it going to be?"

Chris pondered. *That gun probably weighs half a ton . . . and it's lashed to that piece of deck . . .* An idea crashed through the roof of his mind the way new and obvious ideas sometimes do. *That deck is made of wood. Wood floats. All that wood must be helping to float the gun. If only we could get a line on the gun . . .*

In mid-March there came another calm, warm day. The Machias Gun Club rallied at dawn and, with the ebb tide, arrived at the rock about low water to find everything just as they had left it. Chris had a big loose noose of rope weighted with cod sinkers to drag over the muzzle of the gun and then pull tight. After many tries, it failed and caught only a piece of the deck.

"Let's lift it, deck and all," said Chris. They pulled the noose tight, pulled the line as tight as they could over *Alice's* gunnel, and made it fast. As the tide came—and it comes three feet an hour in Machias Bay—*Alice* began to heel. All four lined *Alice*'s free rail, but still she heeled. Suddenly the line came slack. *Alice* heeled the other way, flipping Chris and Dan overboard. They clambered dripping into the boat and found the noose had slipped off the projection on which it had caught.

"But to do that," said Foxy, "it must have tipped up that piece of deck. If we could only get a line on the gun—"

"Let's see the noose," said Chris. He slacked it up a way and began to take off his boots.

"What are you gonna do? You crazy?" chattered Dan, already shivering in his wet clothes.

"The water's cold, but not that cold," said Chris, taking his pants off. "I can stand it for a bit. Pass me the line. Those sinkers will help me down."

"Don't do it," said Jerry. "It's too cold and not worth it."

"You'll freeze your balls off," said Foxy. But Chris took the noose and eased himself breathlessly over the side.

"Give me slack," he gasped, then took several deep, controlled breaths and went under. They saw the white soles of his feet as he went down.

They all held their own breaths anxiously. They could see him stirring about the butt end of the gun.

Then his head burst to the surface and he clung to the side of the boat, gasping and holding the line. All three helped to roll him into the boat. He passed the line to Jerry, and when he could get his breath, said, "Pull on it real easy and slant it to the west." Jerry felt the noose tighten and fetch up on something solid. "You got it?" shivered Chris.

"Got something," said Jerry. "Here, take the line, Foxy, and hold a strain on it. Take my coat, Chris. You must be froze."

"Take mine," said Foxy. "You're my size. Give yours to Dan, Jerry."

"Time to go home," said Chris. They buoyed the line again and started up the river, Chris and Dan rowing to keep warm, but they tired quickly so Jerry and Foxy took the oars. In smooth water and with a fair tide, they got to the Wildcat Inn before dark. Even with a warm fire, dry clothes, and a mug of hot buttered rum, it was some time before heat penetrated to their chilled bones and they stopped shivering.

The next time the Machias Gun Club visited Sheep Island Rock, they took a small log two feet longer than the width of *Alice*. "Pick up the buoy, Dan. Is she still fast to anything?" said Chris. Dan gave a tentative pull and then a heave.

"Sure is," said Dan.

"Then pull it up short." Chris tied a short piece of line around the buoy line as far down as he could reach, carried it around the stern and up the other side. He made it fast to one end of the log lying across *Alice*'s gunnels and bade Dan tie the buoy line to the other end of the log. Now the gun would hang from both ends of the log with no tendency to tip *Alice* over. She would be tiddley though, with the weight high on her gunnels.

"Now we wait for the tide," said Chris.

Meanwhile, Jerry and Foxy had gone off in the bateau, looking along the edge of the rock to the eastward for the other guns. The rock stood high out of the water, now at the bottom of the tide. "Let's get right up on it now," suggested Foxy. Maybe we can see better from high up." There was almost no sea running, the little waves just swishing around the base of the rock. Jerry edged the bateau in gently, stern first, on the north side of the rock. Foxy stepped ashore, climbed to the top, and looked carefully along the north side, especially over toward *Alice*, now beginning to be pulled down by the weight of the gun. Jerry was paddling slowly to the west, along the north side of the rock, peering over the side, his nose practically in the water. After a while, Jerry shouted, "Hooray! I found one! And it's not in very deep water either."

Foxy scrambled to the west end of the rock to be picked up, but Jerry was still looking at his gun. Foxy walked idly along the edge of the water, flushed a lobster out from under a rock, and nearly stumbled over another gun, high and dry on the rock.

"Hey, Jerry, Foxy, get over here quick! We're adrift!" called Chris.

Jerry picked up Foxy and they found *Alice* down to her second plank and the gun with a piece of the deck hanging just clear of the bottom.

"Foxy, take our painter and tow us real easy toward that little beach on the island. Dan, don't you shift that quid to your other cheek or we'll swim again. This rig is some tiddley." Slowly, gently, they crossed the deeper water and came in toward the beach. The gun grounded.

"Tide's still coming," said Chris. "We'll take her in one more jump. What did you fellas find?"

"What did we find, Foxy? What did we find? I'll tell you! Two more guns," exulted Jerry. "One in maybe six feet of water, and one high and dry on the rock."

"Well, it was until the tide came up to it," added Foxy.

"Now what?" asked Dan. "How do we get these monsters up the river?"

"We could take them one at a time in *Alice*, but that would take all summer and we got things to do," said Chris.

"We're adrift again. Haul us in a little closer."

"We need something bigger. We could build a raft."

"How about *Polly*? Has Ike left yet?"

"He wanted to go yesterday, but he waited for a deck load. Trouble is, we'd have to pay him."

"Elect him to the gun club and cut him in for a fifth," suggested Foxy.

"We could try him," said Jerry. "With *Polly*, we could get all four in one load if we could find the other one." The gun had been bumping on bottom as they talked and Jerry had been urging it ahead at each bump, but now the tide had turned and the gun rested solidly on the shingle beach. The lines were coming slack and *Alice* regained her buoyancy. They could see the gun clearly now, lying in about ten feet of water.

"Time to go," said Chris. "She isn't going anywhere and no one's likely to steal her." The Machias Gun Club rowed back up the river against the tide, cheered as much by success as by the chance of gain.

Just before sunset Chris and Dan rounded the bend below town and saw *Polly* still on her mooring with a deckload of cordwood. "*Polly*, ahoy," Chris hailed. Ike poked his head out of the hatch and looked around, rather like a woodchuck on Groundhog Day.

"Oh, it's you, Chris. Come aboard, and you too, Dan." Seated on the lockers in *Polly's* little cabin, mugs in hand, Ike asked, "What have you boys been up to?"

"We've been looking over the wreck of the *Halifax*," said Dan.

"Not much left of her now," said Chris. "Just her two masts and some of her rigging and her guns."

"Her guns?" *That attracted his attention*, thought Chris. "Did you find them?"

"We found three, and the fourth can't be far away."

"What're you going to do with them?"

"We thought you might help us on that, Captain. They're pretty heavy. About maybe half a ton apiece. Now if you'd bring *Polly* down some smooth day when you get back from this trip, we'd—"

"Who's *we?*" broke in Ike.

"The Machias Gun Club. Us two and Jerry and Foxy," said Chris. "While you're gone, we'll find the other gun, get lines on all of them. With some help, we could h'ist all four aboard *Polly* and sail them right up here. Then we could elect you to the Machias Gun Club and divide equally."

"You really did? You found three? And you can find the other? Of course I'll help you. I can see the admiral this trip and I'm sure he'll buy the guns back. They're King George's guns and the admiral will pay salvage. Fill up and we'll drink to the King." Ike poured a small tot all around and because an earlier King had given permission to drink his health afloat without standing, they raised their mugs. "To his Royal Majesty, King George III," intoned Ike.

As they rowed ashore, Dan said, "It sure graveled me to drink to the King, but it was good rum and Ike agreed to fetch the guns."

"Of course he did," said Chris. "It makes him look good with the admiral and the admiral with the King. We all win."

The gun club used every gentle day at the rock when the tide served. As the prospect of success improved, Bill Campbell and Sam Weatherall hastened to join, followed by John O'Brien, Ben Foster, and other Sons of Liberty. They found the fourth gun just under water in a crevice on the south side of the rock and got stout lines to each of the four.

Ike was as good as his word. Ian and Jackie rigged the stoutest hoisting tackle they could find to *Polly's* gaff. After a rough spell of weather, there came a good chance. *Polly* shipped the gun club and a crew of stout woodsmen. Bossed by Ian, and with much "he-o-HEAVE" and "Yo-ho-ho," they got all four guns aboard, sailed gently up the river, and the next day landed the black monsters next to Steve Jones's wharf. They did not look so big, lying high up on the beach at low water.

Reverend Lyon came down to survey the triumph, to observe. "It is wonderful what men can do with God's help," he said with his hand on Chris's shoulder. Judge Jones called it "a monument to courage and persistence," and Glenn went to prepare for the party that he knew was sure to come. After numerous toasts to Jerry, to Foxy, to Dan, to Chris, to Ike, to Jerry's father for being Jerry's father, to Ian for being Chris's father—which most people knew he wasn't—Judge Jones called for quiet and almost got it. Jerry took the floor. "Fellow gunners—nearly every man in Machias now considered himself a member—fellow gunners, we have done close to a miracle here and many of you have helped. It couldn't have been done without you, but without Chris MacDonald it couldn't have been done at all. He it was who wrecked *Halifax* in the first place. He it was who went overboard in icy water in March to secure the first gun. He it was who taught the Fundy tide how to lift that gun to the beach. Now he needs a house, for Ruthie and the twins. You who were quick to join the gun club, will you help Chris now?"

When the chorus of enthusiastic assent died down, Judge Jones adjourned the meeting, but it was late in the night before the last light went out at The Wildcat Inn.

Chapter 23

Concord and Lexington

Early Sunday afternoon, the 24th day of April in 1775, Robbie walked out of the woods and into the kitchen. Alice was clearing away the dinner dishes, a large apron over her Sunday-go-to-meeting dress. Startled, with a wet smash she dropped the earthenware bean pot and gasped, "Where did you come from?"

After assuring her that he was indeed her son Robbie and not a ghost, he asked, "Where is Jerry O'Brien? I have news for him and the Sons of Liberty—important news."

"He's over with your father and Chris, framing up Chris's new house."

"Chris's house? Where's that? Tell me. I can't stop to talk now."

"On the wood road beyond the mill, on the way to East Branch."

Robbie was out the door, down the bank, into a canoe that he found there, leaving Alice shaken, confused and a little frightened. She picked up the broken bean pot and scooped up the beans.

Robbie climbed the far bank, passed the mill, and hailed the three in the framed-up house. "Sons of Liberty, ahoy," he called.

"What's up? How did you get here?" asked Ian.

"Walked over from Chandlers River. Seems the British

soldiers marched out of Boston last Tuesday and killed a lot of our men and we drove 'em back in again. The militia is camped all around—"

"Slow down, Robbie," said Ian. "Begin at the beginning. We know that General Gage dissolved the Massachusetts legislature, which refused to dissolve and set up in Concord as the Provincial Congress and has been governing Massachusetts and raising militia companies."

Robbie continued: "The Congress had collected powder, shot, and a few cannons in Concord and Gage sent a regiment of soldiers out to seize them. The soldiers killed eight men in Lexington, just shot them down, and more in Concord, and we drove them back to Boston and killed a lot of them."

"Who are 'we'?" demanded Chris.

"I'll tell you who *we* are," replied Robbie hotly. "We are citizens of Massachusetts minding our own business and taking no orders from a man in a red coat. Where do you stand in all this? You are a citizen of Massachusetts. Will you let butchers in red coats murder your people?"

There followed a long silence. Chris made no answer. Jerry broke in: "I say we get up a company of the Sons who know what to do with a musket and get ourselves down to Boston quick as we can. You coming, Ian?"

"Just hold your horses, Jerry," replied Ian. A company from Machias should go with the vote of the town behind them. Can you get Ben Foster to call a town meeting right away and vote to raise and supply a company of militia? This should be done legal." Jerry agreed to talk with Ben Foster, to post a warrant on the meeting house door and to talk with Ephraim Chase and Si Weston.

Ian turned to Chris and Robbie. "We'll have to go home and talk this over."

*   ★   ★   ★*

With Alice and Ruthie, they sat around the table in the house that Ian had built, the house in which Albert and John had been born. Slowly and more calmy, Robbie went over the story of Lexington again for his mother and Ruth.

"I will never forget it! The soldiers all lined up across the green, a red line, muskets slanted up, bayonets shining. A rank of our men standing fast. The green speckled with Lexington people running, some with guns, some without. Then the red line, running, shouting, firing. The little line of our men firing and then a terrible mix-up of stabbing and shooting. A British officer on a horse shouting and waving a sword.

"The soldiers lined up again and marched off toward Concord, leaving eight Lexington men dead and others lying on the ground, wounded and in pain. Do you know what a musket ball does to a man? It is about the size of a walnut and solid lead. It smashes whatever it hits. I helped one man hit in the leg. It smashed the bone and everything around it and nearly took his leg off. I stopped the bleeding, but he will lose the leg, and if he survives, will have to stump around the rest of his life on a wooden leg and a crutch."

"Did the soldiers fire first?" asked Ian.

"They did" said Robbie. "I was right there and saw the whole thing. The soldiers fired first and our men had been sternly ordered not to fire unless the British started it. John Parker had even told our men to scatter before the British fired, but they stood fast and did all they could."

"Then why did the soldiers fire?" asked Chris.

"I don't know," said Robbie. "But Chris, you don't understand this war. The soldiers were sent here to put us down, to force us to obey. We refused and prepared to defend ourselves. When those soldiers saw us drawn up in a line with muskets ready, they did what they were trained to do. They shouted, fired and charged with the bayonet."

"What happened after that, Robbie?"

"I don't exactly know. I was tying up arteries and splinting bones, but in the afternoon the redcoats marched back. We heard them coming from the shooting. Minutemen from all the towns around were following them and running along the sides and shooting at them and they were shooting back. We got out of their way, but after they passed through Lexington on the Boston Road, some more soldiers with cannons showed up and protected them. They all went on toward Boston, but our militia kept following them and shooting at them and shooting from behind trees and houses and stone walls. The soldiers burned the houses and killed some of our people, too."

Silence followed. A long silence.

"What is the situation now?" asked Ian.

"I left the next day when I found a sloop bound east, but when I left, militia from all the towns around, Charlestown, Cambridge, Watertown, Milton, were camped around Boston."

"Now, Chris," said Ian gravely, "This is one we can't walk away from. You cannot just mind your own business and shut your eyes to the rest of the country. There is no middle ground, no neutral position. Either you are a loyal subject of King George, whose troops have been attacked by rebels, or you are a loyal American whose people are being attacked by a foreign army. You now must be one or the other. What are you, American or British?

"I'll tell you where I stand," burst in Ruthie. "My people were here when the English first came. They fought for their land and they lost it. The white men lived here, worked here, became Americans, and my mother married the best of them. Now the English are shooting Americans again. We will defend our land this time, and I can shoot a musket."

Chris thought. He thought two ways. *I am not an American. Probably my parents were Spanish. Americans have scorned me all my life for my small size and swarthy skin. But I don't like the British any better. I am not British and I am not American. So the soldiers shot some people. Soldiers do. I'll just keep out of it.*

But what will I do when a barge with fifty British troops and a cannon comes upriver? Welcome them? Surrender? Or . . .

Chris stopped thinking. The love for all that had been his life welled up in him. Alice and Ian and Robbie; Ruthie and the boys; Si and the gun club; the river, the hills, the salt marsh, and the open sea. These were not pictures or ideas. Love flooded him. He knew that he was an American. He knew now where he stood. All the people he loved were Americans. They deserved a free country and he would fight to win it with them. It had been a long silence.

"I'm with you, Pa," he gasped. Ruthie hugged him hard and, with tears in his eyes, he embraced Ian, Alice, and Robbie.

"I think I must have known it all the time," said Chris.

Three days later, about noon on Wednesday, April 27, a gull flying over Machias might have thought every man in town was being drawn to the meeting house by an invisible thread. They came from the mills, from the store, out of the wood roads, and from the East Branch. They came in hay wagons from the ricks in the salt marsh, from houses, barns, and the hovels that sheltered the oxen. They came from the spar shop and from the new house in frame to crowd into the meeting house for one of the most important town meetings in the short history of Machias.

Ben Foster rapped with a mallet on a table at the front of the room. After a good deal of rustling and the tag ends of dying conversations, Ben proclaimed, "This meeting will come to order. The first item on the warrant is to elect a moderator."

"I move Judge Jones be moderator."

"Second."

"Are there other nominations?" Ben asked, knowing there would be none.

"All in favor of Judge Jones for moderator."

There was a chorus of "aye"s.

Judge Jones took the mallet, now a gavel, from Ben and assumed his official position behind the table. He called on the Reverend Lyons to open the meeting with a prayer. He did, and concluded with, "Amen." This was all very formal and legal and had been adopted word for word from the town meeting in Scarborough, from which most of the families in Machias had come.

"The next article on the warrant is to see if the town will raise and equip a company of men to join other Massachusetts militia in defending our liberties. The chair recognizes Jerry O'Brien."

"I move the article as written," said Jerry.

"Second," said Ed Weston.

Jerry continued, "You have all heard by now of the battle at Lexington and Concord. Robbie MacDonald was there and he told you how the British soldiers, for no reason at all, shot down and killed eight men of the Lexington militia and marched off, leaving ten more men badly wounded and in pain. You have heard how one man crept to the door of his house and died on his own doorstep.

"But the Minutemen turned out from Concord and other towns and drove those soldiers back to Boston, shooting them down from behind walls and trees and houses. We have shown them that Massachusetts men don't have to suffer being murdered and robbed by British soldiers. We can beat them back to where they came from."

The room erupted in cheers. Judge Jones rapped his gavel sternly.

"Order! The chair recognizes Owen Johnson."

"No one cherishes liberty more than I do," said Owen, standing. "But consider, friends, the position we occupy in America. We are a timber town. We live by cutting, sawing, and selling our timber, which is taken to Boston and traded for everything we need to survive. Consider that our enemies, if we make them our enemies, can very easily cut off that trade and leave us here in the far corner of Massachusetts to subsist on clams and—sawdust."

Old Morris O'Brien sprang to his feet unrecognized by the chair and burst out, "The British drove us from Scotland so they could run sheep. They drove us from Ireland, but by God they ain't going to drive us out of here. I say fight 'em and fight 'em now.

More shouting and Judge Jones pounded the gavel. "Order! The meeting will come to order. The chair recognizes Ephraim Chase."

"Lots of us have gardens," said Ephraim. "We have cows and pigs and chickens, not enough yet; but we have cleared a lot of land and we can farm it. We can build a vessel and carry our shooks and barrel staves and deals to the West Indies and sell them there for twice what they will bring in Boston. We are not helpless. We don't have to lie down and roll over for a boatload of lobster backs."

"The chair recognizes Eben Murray."

"Raising and supporting a company of men will be expensive for the town. Each man must have powder and shot, a blanket, enough rations to get him to Boston at least. We have no idea who is commanding the militia there, if anyone is. We don't know if they are being issued rations. We don't know what is happening. I move we table the motion until we have more information."

"Hear him! Hear him!" There were a few boo's and hisses.

"Hearing no second, the chair recognizes Stephen Jones."

"I run the store. I have about a month's supply of provisions for the town," said Jones. "No doubt some of you have a little more squirreled away. But this is no time to start a farm. We have a good connection with Boston through my Uncle Ike. He seems to have a good market for lumber and a way of getting supplies for the store out of Boston or Salem. Let's not disturb a working plan. A company of our soldiers, if they could get to Boston, would put us back to clams and lobsters in a month."

"The chair recognizes Ben Foster."

"We have to do *something!*" Our people have been shot down, murdered; but we have shown that Massachusetts militia are quick to act in their own defense and are not afraid of a red coat and a high hat. I suggest that we pass the article to show that we are committed to this course and then send someone straight off to Massachusetts to see if the militia has indeed shut up the British in Boston, who is in command, and how our company could be of the most use. Let the messenger return quickly and we will be ready to send a company at once."

A voice from the floor called out, "How do you like clams and beach peas? We have tried that once."

"Sons of Liberty, vote! Vote and march on Massachusetts!"

Judge Jones hammered his gavel to quell the rising tumult. "Order," he shouted, "order!"

"Let the meeting come to order." Quiet was at last established. "Those in favor of the motion to raise a company will stand." The Sons of Liberty stood. A few others hesitantly came to their feet, looked around at who was not standing, and sat down again. The Judge counted. "Those opposed." Again the Judge counted. "The 'Nay's have it. The motion fails."

Chris jumped to his feet, shouting, "We have to do something! If we can't tell the British and 'specially the Massachusetts Congress where we stand, if we don't back up our own people, we are cowards. I move that we at least set up a liberty pole *now* to tell the British and this town and every other town in Massachusetts that we stand for freedom and the right to mind our own business."

There were more cheers and stamping of feet, rising to pandemonium. The judge gaveled and shouted "Order!", but in vain. People were already moving out the door. Judge Jones turned to Ben and, aware that no one else could hear him, said in an ordinary voice, "Ben, I believe the ayes have it by acclamation. This meeting is adjourned."

That afternoon, willing hands dug a deep hole on the knoll below the mill. Others, guided by Ian, selected a tall, straight spruce, cut it down in short order, trimmed off the branches except for a plume at the top. Twenty men lifted it shoulder high, marched to the hole, and planted it firmly on the knoll. They stamped the soil down hard around it, confident that they had done good work in the name of freedom.

Chapter 24

War

The next morning, Judge Jones let it be known that he was accepting enlistments in the company of the Machias Minutemen. During the following days, about thirty-five men signed up, including Jerry and John O'Brien, Big Dan and Foxy of the gun club, Ian, Chris, Ben Foster, Ephraim Chase, and Ed Weston. Robbie set off for Boston to gather information. At the first muster, Judge Jones was elected captain and Ben Foster, lieutenant. Ben commanded the thirty-five soldiers to come to attention, which they did willingly enough, but clumsily.

"We all know how to shoot a musket, give us time," said Ben. "But we don't know how to act together and to act quickly. Every other day an hour before sunset, we will meet here and learn how to act on the word of command."

"Ben, when're we going to Boston?"

"When we can act like soldiers. All we could do now is add to the confusion. We'll wait 'til Robbie gets back and tells us where we can do some real good."

The soldiers drilled regularly. Although they had not enough powder for extensive firing practice, they learned to form ranks, march together, and obey orders promptly. They went through the motions of loading their muskets and firing on command. They had no uniforms, but just their soldierly appearance attracted recruits and swelled their numbers to forty.

In the second week of May, a sloop set Robbie ashore at Bucks Harbor. He walked home and soon gathered an audience at the inn.

"I walked into Cambridge, and the place is a sculch. Companies are camped wherever they can find an open place. I did see a few tents and some of the companies have moved into houses the Tories have abandoned, but most of them had shelters made of old sails or brush and boards and slept on the ground."

Robbie went on in some detail about the militia he had seen, "A few had uniforms either left from the French war or local militia uniforms, but most were wearing the clothes they had stood up in a month ago. They were dirty, ragged, unkempt, most unmilitary. The Provincial Congress has almost no money and little food. Towns sent in food for their own men and through barter, generosity, or thievery, some others got enough to eat. Dr. Warren and Israel Putnam, a colonel from Connecticut, were getting some order into the chaos. Putnam's company and a company under Arnold are uniformed and well drilled. General Artemus Ward, from somewhere out near Worcester, is said to be in command, but most of his soldiers have yet to see him. For the most part, confusion reigns," Robbie concluded. "Nevertheless, we are keeping the British penned in Boston."

"Robbie," asked Jerry, "where would our company be most useful?"

"Not just yet, Jerry. Let things settle down a little and they'll be very glad to see us. Wait a bit."

They had not long to wait. On June 2, two sloops and a schooner sailed up the river. The sloops were Ike's, *Polly* and

Unity, loaded with supplies for the store. The schooner was HM Armed Schooner *Margueritta,* commanded by Midshipman James Moore. He had passed his examination for lieutenant and was only waiting to be promoted by assignment to a ship that mounted carriage guns. *Margueritta* carried only swivel guns firing a ball little larger than a musket ball and mounted on the rail. His orders from Admiral Graves were to convoy Jones's sloops to Machias, to see that Jones loaded lumber for the building of barracks, to bring back the guns salvaged from *Halifax,* and to see that Jones did indeed return to Boston with the lumber.

Polly anchored a half-mile down river. *Unity* came alongside the store wharf, and *Margueritta* anchored just below the falls in front of the town. The first man ashore was Captain Ike, master of *Unity.* He told those gathered on the wharf that he had a considerable quantity of provisions in his two sloops and that he intended to return to Boston with cargoes of lumber.

"Lumber for what?" asked Jerry O'Brien sharply.

"Barracks for lobster backs," broke in his brother John. General murmurs rose up from the Minutemen, but just then Captain Moore strode up. The master of a British naval vessel is by courtesy called captain regardless of his rank. Moore was obviously in a hurry, but seemed a bit nervous, too.

"Mr. Jones, I understand you have the 3-pounders salvaged from the *Halifax.* Would it not be well before we start dealing in beef and rum to deal with the guns? I have been ordered to bring them to Boston."

"Certainly, Captain Moore. You will find them just below high-water mark on the east side of this wharf. I understand that you have been authorized to pay salvage for them."

"Within a reasonable limit, sir."

"Would fifty pounds settle the account?"

"Four guns at ten pounds is forty pounds," replied Captain Moore.

"But, sir," returned Jones, "there were five men involved in the salvage. Five men at ten pounds each is fifty pounds. It seems to me that King George would pay a man ten pounds for several days of hard work in very cold water for a gun that would cost much more than that to cast. I think, sir, fifty pounds is a fair price and would be acceptable to these gentlemen."

With some twenty determined men surrounding him, Captain Moore replied, "Since you put it that way, I am sure his gracious Majesty would be glad to reward his loyal subjects generously. If you will do me the honor of visiting my schooner, we will conclude the matter at once. I will tell off a party to bring the guns aboard." Moore and Jones went off together, Moore glad to have the guns at any price and Jones glad to have ten pounds for himself and ten for each member of the gun club.

Steve Jones took charge of the supplies on the wharf, some of which had already been unloaded from *Unity*. He held a board with a large piece of paper tacked to it. "This says," he announced, " 'I swear not to interfere in any way with the loading of lumber in the sloops *Unity* and *Polly* and will defend their owner and crews from all harm that may threaten them.' You will have to sign this to do business with the store."

"Who says so?" demanded Ed Weston.

"Captain Jones says so, and he owns the supplies," answered Steve.

"There's some others might have something to say," said Ed.

"Quite a number will have something to say," said Eben Murray. "We are a law-abiding town and a law-abiding people.

We have been since we started here and we want to keep on that course. Ike Jones helped us start this town. Now if some people don't want to sign this paper, let's have a proper legal town meeting and decide whether our town will sell timber to Ike or not."

"Monday, mid-morning," called Selectman Ben Foster.

Captains Jones and Moore, their business concluded, came on deck and contemplated the peaceful town of Machias, the sawmills quiet for the moment.

"That is my mill," said Ike, pointing out the sights of Machias. "Down the bank is the Wildcat Inn, the new east wing just visible on the right, and the larger building over there is the church and meeting house, also used as a school room. That building with the long ell is Ian MacDonald's spar shop and—"

"Pray, sir, what is that pine denuded of branches except for a tuft on top? Surely that is not a liberty pole?"

"I am afraid it is, sir."

"It must come down," said Moore, eager to express the authority of the Navy now that he had the guns under hatches.

"You may find that easier said than done," muttered Ike under his breath.

"Mr. Stillingfleet, my boat at once." Moore's second in command, Midshipman Stillingfleet, had the boat alongside with two oarsmen very quickly. The two officers climbed the bank and approached the liberty pole. Some of the Minutemen clustered around.

"This pole must come down today," declared Captain Moore.

"Not so," said John O'Brien. "That pole was planted with

the unanimous approval of the people of Machias."

"Well, sir," replied the officer. "With or without their approval, it is my duty to demand its removal."

"Must come down," repeated O'Brien with an edge to his voice. "Such words are easily spoken, my friend. I think it is easier to make such a demand than it will be to enforce it."

"What? Am I to understand that resistance will be made? Will the people of Machias dare to disregard an order, not originating with me, gentlemen, but from the government whose officer I am?"

"The people of Machias will dare do anything in maintenance of their principles and their rights."

"It is useless to bandy words," rejoined Captain Moore, a little nettled by the determined spirit of the townsfolk. "My orders are peremptory and must be obeyed. That liberty pole must be taken down or it will be my painful duty to fire upon the town." As he turned to get aboard his boat, Ike spoke to him quietly and so urgently that he paused.

"You must be aware, Captain Moore, that you have heard only from a small, radical, and militant faction in the town. Let us call a general meeting tomorrow, which will include sensible property owners and no small number loyal to the King. We can settle this thing legally and without bloodshed."

Moore nodded reluctantly. "Agreed," he said quietly.

Meanwhile the leaders of the Minutemen had gone together up the bank to Ian's spar shop. They agreed to send at once to Pleasant River and Chandlers River for every man who would help in the defense of Machias.

The town meeting was held the next day, Saturday. It was moved without much formality that the liberty pole be removed. The sensible property owners and the Tories, if any were present, were shouted down by a chorus of "No."

Moore was ready to fire on the town, but he had only a few swivel guns mounted on the rails, which were incapable of doing much damage to a town of scattered houses. The 3-pounders were in the hold, as yet unmounted. Still, the act of a British naval vessel firing on an American town would have to be taken seriously. Ike came aboard *Margueritta*.

"Captain Moore, I was at that meeting. It wasn't a meeting; it was a riot. There was no proper discussion. They did not understand that the whole future of a lumber town depends upon a market and that you and I control their access to that market. Furthermore, Admiral Graves would find armed conflict in eastern Maine most unwelcome at this time.

"I suggest that I personally, assisted by my cousin, Judge Jones, call a new meeting on Monday, to be conducted under formal circumstances. I believe that the people of Machias will find that they will prefer to eat than to worship a pine tree. I further suggest that we both attend divine service tomorrow as evidence of our peaceful intentions and see if we cannot cool these hot heads and settle this peacefully."

"All right, I agree," said Moore, "but if that pole is not down one hour after that meeting, I will fire on the town."

Foster ordered his Minutemen to gather Sunday morning before church at the edge of the woods. He posted sentries to meet the volunteers from Chandlers River and Pleasant River and to direct them to the rendezvous. John O'Brien and Big Dan volunteered to hold Moore and Jones in church until the Minutemen arrived. Then they would seize the two sloops and the *Margueritta*.

Ian, Chris, and Robbie turned out early Sunday morning and headed toward the woods. Ian carried his musket and a box of cartridges, a horn of powder slung over his shoulder. Each cartridge was a small paper sack in which was a musket ball and a charge of powder. In action, Ian would tear the sack open, pour the powder down the musket barrel, drop the ball on top of it, stuff the paper in on top of the ball and ram it down hard with the ramrod. He would bang the butt of the musket on the ground to shake some of the powder into the pan, then cock back the hammer to be sure the flint was in place, and fire. Robbie was a formidable adversary, standing a good six feet tall and swinging a double-bladed axe. Chris carried a hatchet, a knife at his belt, and a firm determination in his jaw.

As they approached the trail and crossed a small brook, a number of Minutemen materialized, partly hidden by the new June foliage. There was a strong contingent, too, from the neighboring towns, mostly farmers and woodsmen.

Lieutenant Ben Foster addressed his troops, most of whom had as yet no idea of their mission. "Minutemen and good neighbors, here is our plan. John O'Brien is sitting behind Captain Moore in church and Big Dan behind Ike Jones. John and Dan will seize and hold Moore and Jones and the first squad of Minutemen will go in and tie them up. Another group, Chris, Nat, Ian, and Robbie and you men standing to the left of that oak tree, will go for the shore, unload *Unity* and unbend her sails. You to the right of the oak tree with Jerry and Foxy will run down the river, seize *Polly*—anchored somewhere above the Rim—and bring her up to town. The rest of us will seize *Margueritta* if we can, but that may be more difficult. She has swivel guns and a crew that probably knows how to use them."

"Ben, this attacking a naval officer and seizing a naval vessel is out and out active rebellion, a hanging offense. We are putting our necks in the noose."

"That's right. We are," answered Ben loudly enough so all could hear. "If you are ready to strike for freedom, hanging is the price of failure. The Minutemen of Concord and Lexington took that chance and the chance of stopping a musket ball and the chance of having their houses burned. When you signed up for the Minutemen, you took that chance. Are you with me?"

More than one soldier looked down, shuffled his feet in the dead leaves underfoot, wavered. Chris's heart skipped a beat and he swallowed hard. Ian leaned his musket against a tree, put an arm over each of his sons' shoulders, squeezed a bit, held tight. "We are all in this together, lads," he said.

Ben sensed a general uneasiness. A number of those under his command had not thought this through. He wanted to spend no time in debate and he wanted no half-hearted soldiers. "Those who are with me, cross this brook." He took three steps and leaped. Jerry, Ian, Chris, and Robbie were right behind him. Others followed and they never looked back. They followed Ben toward the church.

Meanwhile, the service had continued much as usual, with prayers and psalms. Reverend Lyons was pretty well into his sermon when Captain Moore, looking out the open window, saw men hurrying toward the church, some with muskets, but all armed in some way. Scattering worshippers, he dove out the window. He rolled when he hit the ground and came up running for the shore. Captain Jones, only a step behind him, struck for the woods.

The militia gave chase, but Moore had a good start and was fast on his feet. His boat with Stillingfleet in charge was waiting for him. As he leaped over the stern, the two oarsmen pulled away. Ben and the leaders of the militia came down the bank to find *Margueritta*'s boat out of range. The rest of the militia came puffing up. Ben turned, climbed the bank, and stood up on a rock. "Squads, go for *Unity* with Chris and for

Polly with Jerry. Others stay here." Chris, Nat, Ian, Robbie, and a dozen others ran for the store wharf. Chris sent a group below to pass cargo to the hatch and detailed others to take it to the store. He, Ian, Robbie, and Nate, the only ones who knew anything about rigging, unbent the sails. Steve Jones arrived breathless from church and tried to keep some kind of order among the barrels and bags. In two hours, *Unity*'s cargo was ashore and her spars bare.

Jerry's party ran down the shore and boarded *Polly*. Jerry confronted the bewildered skipper. "We have come to take this sloop in the name of the Machias Sons of Liberty." The skipper glanced at Jerry's musket and a well-sharpened scythe blade on a pole in the hands of a burly farmer from Chandlers River.

"All right, Jerry," said the skipper, "but let me and my mate ashore. We'll have no part in this piracy."

Jerry mustered a crew, and awkwardly they got sail on her with much expenditure of sweat and bad language. "Hey, you in the stern, let go the main sheet. Not you; the one next to you." The man looked up vacantly at the partly hoisted sail. "The main sheet, you dumb bugger! That rope you're sitting on. Now, you two farmers, pull on these two ropes. Together, you swabs." They managed to pull the anchor and, with Jerry at the tiller, *Polly* headed up the river. She didn't go far. The tide had started to ebb. She tripped on a mud bank, and as the tide left her, she leaned over on her port side, hard aground.

"Josh, you and these four fellas stay aboard and keep off any lobster backs if any come around. You have two muskets and I'll leave you half my powder. The rest of us, we'll go ashore and up the river."

They had not gone far when they saw *Margueritta* coming down with the tide, followed along the bank by Ben and his party, splashing through the edge of the salt marsh. They took occasional musket shots at the schooner and Moore fired back with his swivel guns, but the range was too great.

Margueritta anchored near where *Polly* was hard aground. Hostilities were at a standstill.

After dark, Ben mustered his forces again. The tide had ebbed, so the militia could go out on the flats and get closer to *Margueritta,* but she was just a form in the gloom, a poor target. The gunners on the schooner were shooting against a wooded shore illuminated only briefly with a musket flash. Moore, seeing nothing to gain by shooting at trees, cut his anchor line and dropped down the river with the last of the ebb, tying up alongside a sloop waiting for the flood tide in the morning.

Chris set watches for his crew aboard *Unity*. Some he released to go home, for no action seemed imminent. Ben had found Jerry, John O'Brien, Big Dan, Ephraim Chase, and Ian. They gathered at Ian's house.

"What we ought to do," said Ian, is get *Unity* under way at once and sail down and take *Margueritta*. She has no very big crew and we can take her by boarding her."

Ben added, "With another vessel we'd have him between us. *Falmouth Packet* lies in the East Branch. I can have her here in the morning." There was enthusiastic agreement, so Ben rallied up a crew and marched for the East Branch.

Chapter 25

The Battle of Machias

At first light, Captain Moore got underway with a fair northwest breeze on the first of the ebb tide. Standing by the binnacle on his little quarterdeck, he said to Miles Stillingfleet, "I'm glad we got clear away out of that hornet's nest."

"We could have stayed and got *Polly*, and covered our men with our swivels," suggested Miles.

"Maybe, but how would the Admiral feel about another bloody engagement like Concord? And we are no company of trained marines, but a handful of pressed men." Stillingfleet wisely held his tongue.

"Jibe O," shrieked the man at the tiller. The main boom was rising as if for the coming blow and swept across the deck with the weight of the wind behind it. It fetched up on the main sheet with a crash and a clatter. It was more than a clatter, for the main boom had broken short off about three feet from the mast and one jaw of the gaff had broken. The sail, like a broken wing, was doing the best it could, but it was no rig to carry to Boston.

Captain Moore saw no chance of repairing either spar quickly, but he noticed a sloop at anchor ahead. "All hands," he called, but there was no need to attract their attention. "Get the mainsail off her and unbend it at head and foot. Step lively. Helmsman, lay me alongside that sloop. Mr. Stillingfleet, load your port swivels." Under foresail and staysail, *Margueritta* sailed slowly down on the sloop." Mr. Stillingfleet, fire a shot over his head and not very far over it either." The crews of both sloops lined the rails. *Margueritta* luffed alongside. "Make fast alongside," called Moore. "Captain, come aboard." The captain of the sloop, a short man with gray hair, climbed over the rails and faced Moore.

"Your name, sir," said Moore.

"Avery, William Avery."

"Very well. Unbend your mainsail and put your boom and gaff aboard this vessel."

"Certainly not, sir. You have no right—"

Moore glanced toward the peak of the mainsail, but there was no sail there, no peak and no flag. "My swivels are my warrant, and I don't take back talk from a rebel. Tie him up, you two, and get that boom and gaff over here and bend our mainsail to them."

An hour later, a re-rigged *Margueritta* stood down the bay. Captain Moore, feeling more sure of himself, paced his quarterdeck.

Before the sun was clear of the trees, watchers had found Jerry and told him of *Margueritta's* departure. Jerry ran for the wharf and found Chris and his crew busy bending sails. Jerry mustered a crew to load aboard a small deckload of timbers and passed the word for any who were willing to sail aboard *Unity* to get aboard. John O'Brien and others who had been first across the brook, climbed aboard. As they were setting the mainsail, Joseph Eaton from Pleasant River ran breathlessly up the wharf leading two men carrying heavy bags and two tired young women carrying muskets.

"Hold on," shouted Joe, "we have something you're going

to need. Here's two thirty-pound bags of powder these two girls just lugged through the woods last night. You can't have Hannah and Rebecca, but the powder will do some good."

"Hoist away," shouted Chris, at the tiller. "No time to talk. Come aboard, you fellas, if you want to fight. The girls passed the muskets to Joe and all three men stepped aboard.

Blocks squealed to the "He–O–HEAVE" of the men at the halyards.

"Cast off forward, Nat," called Chris. "Give her staysail and jib. Slack the main sheet, Sam. Way out." *Unity* turned on her heel, held by the stern. "Let go, aft," said Chris, "and make fast the main sheet, Sam."

Unity was on her way on the ebb tide in pursuit of the British schooner. Relieved of her cargo, she slipped quickly down the river, found *Margueritta* gone and *Polly* still hard aground.

"Chris, you keep the tiller," said Jerry. "You know the river. Cut all the corners you can, BUT DON'T GET US AGROUND." What happened to that powder? You two who brought it, get below. Joe, open one bag and serve out to anyone who has a musket."

As they approached the turn where the East Branch joined the river, Chris saw *Margueritta*, not so far ahead as he had feared. He called Nat aft. "We'll have to jibe her on this corner. You take the main sheet. These farmers wouldn't know what to do with it."

Nat took the sheet off the cleat, shouting, "Hey! Everybody get your head down and take hold of something solid."

"Jibe O," called Chris. Nat hauled in the sheet as fast as he could and, with the boom nearly amidships, took two turns around the cleat. The mainsail came over with a heavy jolt as Nat slacked away quickly on the sheet. "Nothing busted," said Chris. "Now, Nat, get forward and see if you can get these farmers to wing out the staysail and jib. Jerry what are you up to?"

"Hadn't you noticed?" said Jerry. "She's firing her swivels at us. One of their slugs splashed just ahead of us. A sort of breastwork of timber would give our soldiers a lot more confidence."

"Better put it just forward of the mast and low enough so the staysail can swing over it," said Chris. John went forward to direct the operation on the crowded foredeck while Chris put his whole attention on getting the best he could out of *Unity*.

After a few minutes, he turned to Ian, who was standing beside him. "Pa, do you think your musket will reach her from here?"

"Dunno. Let's try her." Ian loaded up with a generous charge of powder behind the ball. He fired, and a plume of smoke drifted forward, but no one saw where the shot landed. While they were still looking, a shot from astern snapped their heads around to see Ben Foster's *Falmouth Packet* coming up fast on their port quarter, mainsail out to port, foresail to starboard, and a bone in her teeth.

Margueritta, with her jury-rigged mainsail, was scudding for the open sea, firing her swivels at *Unity*. *Unity* and *Falmouth Packet* pressed ahead, lightened of their cargo and sailed by men who knew their boats and knew the bay. They were fast gaining on *Margueritta*, and as they came within musket range, fire grew hotter and swivel balls slammed into the barricade, sizzled over the heads of the crew, and struck on deck. *Unity* was closing in fast and Chris, concentrating his attention on coming alongside *Margueritta* so his soldiers could board her, paid no heed to the musket balls. He turned to Ian again.

"Pa, do you think you could hit that man at the tiller."

"Might," said Ian.

Ian's musket flashed and the man at the tiller fell. *Margueritta* swung suddenly to port, towards *Unity*. Chris swung *Unity* to starboard, stabbed her bowsprit through *Margueritta*'s mainsail, and locked the two vessels together. John O'Brien fired into the crowd and leaped aboard *Margueritta*. He ran aft to seize the tiller. Two of *Margueritta*'s crew fired at him, missing as he stooped to grab the tiller, and then came for him with cutlasses. He turned and sprang overboard, but Jerry saw him go, threw him a line, and hauled him aboard.

Meantime, *Unity*'s crew charged aboard *Margueritta*. It was a fierce attack, for well-sharpened scythe blades or hand-forged pitchforks are formidable weapons in the hands of determined attackers, and there was neither time nor space to load or fire a musket. *Margueritta*'s crew, some armed with cutlasses and some quite unarmed, fled forward before the fierce-eyed farmers. Captain Moore stood on *Margueritta*'s rail, throwing grenades into the men still struggling to board from *Unity*'s foredeck. There was another shock and a heavy jolt as *Falmouth Packet* slammed alongside *Margueritta*'s starboard bow and another band of fierce farmers took her defenders in the rear. Captain Moore fell back, badly wounded and Stillingfleet clutched a useless arm. Without leadership and beset fore and aft, *Margueritta*'s crew fled below.

Suddenly, there was no one to fight. After the shouting, clashing, and musket shots, suddenly—silence. But it wasn't really silence. Urgent cries of pain came from wounded men, accompanied by the slatting of sails and the bumping and slamming of the three vessels rolling together. Jerry and a squad of his men secured the sailors below. Robbie bent over Captain Moore, using his knife to cut up a shirt for a bandage. Captain Avery was dead, hit by a stray musket ball.

Ian and Nat cast off *Falmouth Packet* and, under Ben Foster, she started back up the bay. Chris and Foxy disentangled *Margueritta* and *Unity*. Chris sailed *Margueritta* up the bay and Nat followed in *Unity*. Captain Foster, seeing the other two under way, fired three shots in salute. Stillingfleet came on deck and surrendered to Jerry, ending the first naval battle of the American Revolution.

Epilogue

When *Unity, Polly,* and *Margueritta* anchored off the town, the biggest and wildest celebration that the Wildcat Inn had ever seen gathered momentum. The volunteers from the neighboring towns joined in enthusiastically. It was rum and rebellion, emphasized by frequent musket shots!

But not everyone was celebrating. Captain Avery and a dozen others were dead. The wounded were suffering, despite care from loving families. Captain Moore, in great pain from his cruel stomach wound, lay on a pallet watched over by Ruthie as he weakened. Moore had been mortally wounded and would die two days later, despite all Robbie could do.

Ben, Jerry, Chris, and Ian speculated, "What will Admiral Graves do about this? Or the vessels in Halifax? If they send a ship loaded with marines to punish us, what can we do?"

"They won't find it easy to punish us if we all stand together."

Like the sudden heavy crash of a breaking wave, Chris realized that they would all stand together. Ian born in Scotland, Alice born in Portsmouth, Robbie born in Kennebunk, Ruthie born in Townsend; yes, and John and Albert born in Machias; and he, himself, wherever he was born—he knew they were all Americans now and would all stand together.

Glossary of Terms

Binnacle: The upright, cylindrical stand holding a ship's compass.

Boom: A spar extending from a mast to hold the bottom of a sail outstretched.

Bowsprit: A large, tapered spar extending forward from the bow of a sailing ship, to which stays for the masts are secured.

Brig: A two-masted ship with square-rigged sails.

Caulk: To seal the cracks and seams of a boat.

Capstan: A rotating spindle around which cables or lines are wound to hoist anchors or lift other weights.

Coaming: A raised border around a hatchway or roof opening to keep out water.

Fo'c's'le: *Forecastle:* The upper deck of a ship in front of the foremast.

Forestay: A rope or cable reaching from the head of a ship's foremast to the bowsprit, for supporting the foremast.

Forestaysail: A triangular sail set from the forestay.

Gaff: A spar or pole extending from the after side of a mast and supporting a fore-and-aft sail.

Gunnel: *Gunwale:* The upper edge of the side of a vessel.

Halyard: A rope or tackle for raising or lowering a flag or sail.

Jib: A triangular sail secured to a stay forward of the mast or foremast.

Luff: *n:* the foreward edge of a fore-and-aft sail. *v:* to turn the bow of a ship toward the wind. To flutter: said of a sail that is heading too close to the wind.

Mainmast: The principal mast of a vessel.

Mainsail: In a square-rigged vessel, the sail set from the main yard. In a fore-and-aft-rigged vessel, the large sail set from the after side of the main mast.

Reef: The part of a sail that can be rolled up or folded to reduce the area exposed to the wind, as during a storm.

Sculch: New England variation of "culch:" A natural bed for oysters, consisting of gravel or crushed shells to which the oyster spawn may adhere. Slangily it's a rubbish heap.

Scupper: An opening in a ship's side to allow water to run off the deck.

Shallop: A small open boat fitted with oars or sails or both.

Snotter: The short line supporting the butt of the sprit in a small boat.

Spanker: A fore-and-aft sail, usually hoisted on a gaff, on the after mast of a square-rigged vessel. The after mast and its sail on a schooner-rigged vessel of more than three masts.

Spindrift: Spray blown from a rough sea or surf.

Sprit: A pole or spar extended diagonally upward from a mast to topmost corner of a fore-and-aft sail, serving to extend the sail.

Stay: A heavy rope or cable used to brace or support a mast.

Staysail: A triangular, fore-and-aft rigged sail fastened on a stay.

Tack: To change the course of a vessel by turning its bow into and across the wind. To sail against the wind by a series of zigzag movements.

Taffrail: The rail around the stern of a ship.

Tiller: A bar or handle for turning a boat's rudder.

Topsail: In a square-rigged vessel, the square sail next above the lowest sail on a mast. In a fore-and-aft-rigged vessel, the small sail set above the gaff of a fore-and-aft sail.